Short Stories

Poetry &

One Hot Essay

A Letter to the Future

If sorrow and angst fill your heart when death invades your mind, remember; all of us sooner or later will pass that way. It is the only road to eternal peace. Your children and grandchildren will be no exceptions. They too will one day face the same pain you now know—the pain of leaving the people you cherish—the pain of knowing you won't be there to comfort them when their time to pass comes—to ease their fear of the uncertain journey that awaits—the fear of no longer being connected to the hearts and minds in the sentient consciousness of those they know and love and will also leave behind.

Teach your children well—encourage them to teach their children well. Don't be dismayed. The veil we pass through is no more than the breath of a shadow. I will wait for you on the other side. Look close; you will see my hand; it reaches back for you through the shadowed veil to unmask the charlatan death.

Sincerely—Roderick E. Billette

Contents

SHORT STORIES

Miriam's Malady

My mother, Miriam, was born with a genetically-mutated gene. A misaligned chromosome is the definitive medical diagnosis, and she unfortunately or fortunately, depending on your point of view, passed it on through her DNA, to my niece, Sheila and my daughter, Joy. I watched Momma and those who got too close to her, in particular, suffer immense pain from time to time and now, I see history repeating itself over and over with Sheila and Joy.

It is an acute and addictive illness with no known cure. Science has scarcely begun to understand its seriousness and how dangerous it is to those infected and also how treacherous it can be to those who happen to come into contact with the sufferer.

Many times, those in close proximity have far more to fear from the malady than the victim. In fact, folks standing or sitting close by are far more likely to endure injury from the disorder than the person who must, through no fault of their own, continue to bear up under the embarrassment of continually losing control of their coordination and muscle function.

This insidious infirmity affects young and old alike and can manifest itself without conscious thought at any age even if it has lain dormant for years. It is more pronounced in some humans than others and until one has been thoroughly tested, there is no way to accurately ascertain to what degree a person might suffer.

What is known is that it is affected by certain human habits, chiefly those around water, boats, and docks, and nearly always when the afflicted person is in possession of a cane fishing pole. The hundred-dollar scientific Latin name is Tossafishonia (TOOFISHI) and the only way to know for sure if you are a carrier is to put a minnow or wriggling worm on a line, hook a fish, watch the bobber disappear, and bravely see how you react.

For most of my first twelve years, I had overheard rumors concerning the seriousness of Momma's illness, but the gravity of her situation did not come to my full attention until one bone-chilling February night on Lake Carlton.

Momma stood with a cane pole in her hand and patiently hummed an old Redback Hymn under her breath. Frosty steam rode into the inky, starlit background under a brightly lit, gas-vapor light on Uncle Adolph's dock. Bright orange, oblong corks rocked gently on the wind-rippled water. From time to time, between stifled yawns, we raised our poles to check on the wriggling minnows we used for bait.

Daddy and Uncle Adolph stood nearby under their caps, hands deep in their pea coat pockets, and talked about the pound/solid price of juice oranges, occasionally cupping their hands together and blowing on them for warmth—no shortage of hot air surrounded that conversation.

The fish were slow to bite on this particular night, and complacency had begun to settle in to our cold and ever-stiffening joints when, of a sudden, Momma's cork went under. A shrill, unearthly scream ran past her lips. She wildly jerked her twelve-foot cane pole out of a ten-foot-deep fishing hole, straight up into the air and slung a poor speckled perch, flailing on the barbed end, directly over her head toward an unsuspecting Uncle Adolph. Her illness had struck.

This display of energy and enthusiasm can be very effective for landing a fish provided no one else is in the vicinity. However, what happens if the fish comes loose from the hook on the backswing? Now you have a naked, razor-sharp barb traveling at a high rate of speed in the hands of an irrational person suffering from TOOFISHI. A dangerous situation as you can easily imagine. A few of my caps and jackets have been victimized over time, but my person has remained unscathed, knock on wood.

Unfortunately, Uncle Adolph, who turned to look in Momma's direction at exactly the wrong moment can no longer claim to be so lucky. The fish Momma had on flew off back into the water, but the hook continued straight and true. It caught the inside of Uncle Adolph's bottom lip, mid-sentence. I mean, it hooked him good!

Uncle Adolph is a Christian man known to never swear, but his religion was sorely tested that night. He muttered something unintelligible over his blood-soaked lip. What he said exactly is hard to tell, but since in my mind he couldn't be understood, he passed the curse test—barely. In a slow, ponderous drawl he somehow reassured and scolded Momma at the same time:

"I do declare, Miriam, I wish you women would pay a more attention to what you're hookin'."

Daddy cut the barbed end of the hook out of Uncle Adolph's mouth with his whet-sharpened, Case pocket knife, no permanent harm done. I have since taken notice that neither of them have ever stood behind Momma again when she has a cane pole in her hand.

Sad to say, Momma never outgrew her condition (it only worsened with time). And since a cure was never found for her malady she continued to prove a real danger to the unsuspecting and uninitiated on the multitude of lakes and rivers around the state of Florida for many years.

And then there was the poor, unwary, North Carolina soul minding his own business—fishing a sparkling trout stream with a fly rod one minute, and having a feathered hook removed from his left nostril by a country doctor the next.

Momma fishes in Heaven now but be fair-warned all you braggarts and liars who loiter around boats, docks and fishing holes, if you see my niece Sheila or my daughter Joy with a cane pole in their hands approach at your own risk. The TOOFISHI malady is dangerous and contagious and if you don't pay attention you'll likely to find yourself on the wrong end of a sharp barb.

Dedicated to the memory of my mother:

Miriam Miley Eaton Billette

Joe Human

On a steep hillside near an American town—it's not important which American town, only that this particular town is near the sea where the incoming flow of moist air lifts fog banks and pushes them regularly inland to snuggle against the rocky earth. In the west such a hillside would be a mere knoll on a high plateau while in the east it is known as a mountain.

What is important, is that the pilot is a real hero whose real last name is Dinwiddie has always preferred to be called Joe Human since ditching his plane. Dinwiddie is too similar to dimwit and Joe is cracked and he knows it—knows it because he overheard the Navy doctor say so after he was shot down in the Pacific a few years back—just how many years ago he can't recall.

The only things Joe is sure of are his ability to pilot an aircraft with unerring skill—the altimeter in his plane never varies—three thousand five hundred feet—and that he is a human being.

Joe lives in a two-story barracks on five hundred acres of prime cattle land with his grandson Bob and his wife Jill. His room is situated so that the enemy could never surprise him and abscond with his aircraft which sits on a nearby hill.

Of course, the way his grandson has secured Joe's pride and joy with anchors and wires, it could only be removed from its present position with great difficulty and bolt cutters. He is assured in that knowledge. The other small difficulty is that the propeller for the airplane has been in the shop for repairs for quite some time.

"Dad?" "Dad?" Jill's voice is insistent. "Can you hear me, Colonel? It's mess time. Come on down, we don't want to eat without you."

Joe loves the promotion. When he was lying in a raft in the Pacific he was sure his wing man had called him Lieutenant. "I'm coming, I'm coming." He swings his skinny legs over the side of his bunk and for a brief moment a flash of cognizance causes him to say, "What the hell, how'd I get here?" The thought quickly fades and leaves him shuffling for the top of the stairs. "I'm coming."

Joe joins his grandson at the barrack's dining table while Jill bustles about pulling a pot roast from the oven. The table, a simple rectangular slab of maple Joe had cut and finished in his woodworking shop five years before, is set with cloth napkins, polished silverware, and exquisite china—the Colonel insists on eating meals in a civilized manner.

Jill places the heavy cast-iron pot in the center of the table and joins her men. "Grandpa, would you please give thanks for our bounty?"

The trio joins hands. The Colonel prays, "Heavenly Father, bless the hands that prepared this food and help us to victory in our fight to defeat the enemy. Amen."

Bob commends his grandfather, "That was a very nice prayer, Colonel. Which enemy do you mean? Pass me your plate. Do you want potatoes and carrots with your roast beef?"

Joe gives his grandson a sideways look. "You know what enemy I'm talking about."

"Yes, I suppose I do."

"Well, quit asking foolish questions and put plenty of that gravy on my potatoes. And don't get any of those damned onions mixed in. You know they give me gas."

Jill laughs. "Grandpa—I mean Colonel, don't you think you ought to be a little more careful with that colorful language. There is a lady present."

Before Joe can reply, Bob chimes in, "I was thinking, Colonel, that after lunch we ought to go into town and get our ears lowered. We're both beginning to look a little shaggy. You don't want to get caught on the parade grounds looking disheveled, do you?"

"I agree one hundred and ten percent, son." Joe lowers his fork and rubs his chin and the sides of his face. "And I could stand a good close shave as well."

Bob winks at his wife. "Then it's settled, Colonel. We'll take the old jeep into town after lunch. Do you mind if Jill rides along on reconnaissance? She needs to resupply at the PX?"

Joe gives an approving nod. "As long as she realizes the danger she's in and keeps her head down. I don't want an enemy sniper taking a pot shot at her. By the way, do you think that barber fellow, Ralph, has gotten any new Popular Mechanic magazines in since we were there last?"

An hour later in town, Ralph, the barber, greets the Colonel with a customary salute. "How are you today, sir?" He brushes off the seat of one of the two barber's chairs in his shop and motions for Joe to be seated. "I've got your special chair waiting Colonel."

Joe nods in his direction as he turns in a confused circle. "Just a damn minute; where are those magazines you keep hidden so well?"

"You mean the Popular Mechanics?"

8

"No, you insubordinate bastard, I mean Good Housekeeping—what do you think I mean? I'll have you brought up for court-marshal with that smart talk"

Ralph exhibits great patience and respect. "I'm sorry, Colonel, I didn't mean to be insubordinate. It won't happen again." He points to a stack of magazines on a corner table. "The brand-new issue of Popular Mechanic is on top. I think you'll find it informative. There's a special section on propellers."

Joe's crinkled, creased eighty-nine-year-old blue eyes light up. "Excellent, excellent, that's the issue I've been waiting for. I'll be back in action in no time at all."

Ralph and Bob wink at each other simultaneously. Bob says, "Maybe you can construct a propeller in your workshop for that P-51 Mustang you've got parked on the hillside, Colonel?

Joe replies, "My thoughts exactly—that Rolls Royce Merlin 60 engine still roars like a lion." He takes a creaky seat in the barber's chair and props his size thirteen military issued boots on the metal footrest. "Now then, let's get this haircut over and done. I've got a lot of work to do when I get back to headquarters." He pauses and looks back sheepishly at Ralph. "That is, you won't mind if I borrow this book?" He holds out the periodical. "It's for the war effort you know?"

Ralph airs out a striped sheet and wraps it snugly around Joe's neck. "Be my guest Colonel—anything to defeat the evil Axis." He winks at Bob again. "You'll save us all yet and we'll be forever in your debt." He runs his comb through Joe's thick white hair and lifts it between two fingers and begins to snip, snip. Then thinks better of his sarcasm "Colonel, I owe you an apology—we're already in your debt.

"That's mighty nice of you to say, son." Joe smiles—he doesn't mind; he has a plan. "Just you remember this smart ass: ain't no winners in war, only lessons forgot, and heroes remembered."

9

The barber finishes Joe's shave and haircut and holds the mirror up for him to review his ruggedly handsome face. "Not bad, not bad." He turns to his grandson. "I'll wait on the bench out front if you don't mind." He pulls a pair of reading glasses from his shirt pocket. "I've got some research to do. Besides, I can keep a clear lookout for ©Jill and any enemy spies skulking about."

He lifts his long slender frame from the chair and walks briskly toward the front door holding tightly to his Popular Mechanic magazine. He waves it high in the air over his shoulder. "See you outside."

Ralph says to Bob, "Well, take a seat, it's your turn. You don't think your grandpa could actually build a working propeller, do you?"

Bob chuckles, "Of course not; do you know what kind of time and precision that kind of project would take? The old man doesn't have the tools or concentration to do that, but it will keep him occupied for a long, long time."

"Does he ever remember what happened to him?"

"Careful with those shears; I came in for a trim not a scalping."

Ralph replies, "Sorry, I was thinking about the stories that have circulated over the years about your grandpa and his warplane."

"Until my father, his only son, J. D., was shot down over Vietnam he wasn't quite as bad." Bob adjusts himself in the chair. "He already suffered from PTSD, but after that he went totally over the edge and insisted on flying reconnaissance to look for him. The only thing we could think to do to keep him going was to situate his plane on that slope—remove the propeller, keep the tires aired, the tanks full, and the engine serviced, so he could sit in the pilot's seat and pretend."

"Why go to so much trouble?" Ralph flips the switch and his shears begin to hum. "He'd probably be content to go sit in his aircraft without the motor running anyway."

10

Bob leans back and relaxes. "You obviously don't know the old man as well as you think you do."

Ralph continues to work on Bob's hair as he comments, "What do you mean?"

"What I mean is, he walks around that plane and does a thorough pre-flight inspection the way the military trained him to every time before he climbs into the cockpit. Let me see that mirror." He points at cluttered sink area.

Ralph passes the hand-held mirror to Bob.

Bob inspects the back of his head in the large wall mirror mounted above the shelf full of talc and tonic water. "I told you; I only wanted a trim."

Ralph takes the mirror back. "Yes Sir." And then continues to buzz behind Bob's ears. "You know it's quite a sight to see your grandpa in that airplane." At last satisfied with his work the barber backs away and shuts his shears off. "There that ought to do it. Everybody around has witnessed the scene. It's quite the sight to see the Colonel in his flak jacket and leather helmet and gloves climb into that cockpit and go off to war. And it's easy to see from his posture and swagger that he was a real-deal pilot."

Bob shakes his head. "When the fog banks roll in I believe he genuinely feels as though he's airborne and flying through the clouds. I often wonder what he thinks about with that engine roaring and the wind whipping about in his face."

Ralph yawns and begins to unwind the protective cloth from around his client's throat. "I'll bet he thinks he's nineteen and it's nineteen forty-five and that he's alive." He pulls the striped sheet off Bob's chest and shakes the shorn hair out on the otherwise spotless black and white tile floor. "Alright you can step down now. You're as pretty as I can make you and that ain't very."

Bob smiles and reaches into his pocket. Ralph puts a hand on his arm. "Not today." He points at the Colonel sitting on the bench reading intently, his lips moving with his mind. "Your family has paid enough. Take good care of your grandpa and we'll call it even."

~

Alaweed bin Faelal, the heir to a vast industrial Middle East fortune, bolts upright, his bedding and clothes soaked in cold sweat. He clamps both hands hard against his head. The nightmares are coming more often, not less often, as he had been led to believe by the American doctors.

The nightmare is always the same. He is huddled with his younger brother and two sisters in the basement of the family home crying and trembling with fear—praying to Allah for deliverance. They hear sirens in the distance. Bombs shake the ground. The atmosphere explodes.

In less than a breath he is flung up and back against the stone wall and the world around him has become eerily silent and wet. There are no screams, only silence and confusion. He strokes his little sister's face and reassures her all will be well. Her eyes stare back at him— blank—unresponsive—far away, already fixed in Paradise.

Alaweed blinks furiously trying to concentrate. He must help his sister. Then he realizes that her body is lying three feet away and he is holding only her sweet face and the wet he feels are her brains and blood. He screams and is still screaming when he is pulled from the rubble two days later.

He vows revenge on the Infidel. He has a plan. He needs a nuclear device. Paradise waits. Allah, Akbar.

~

Short, swarthy, hawk-nosed Akhmed Hashmi finishes briefing his boyhood friend, Alaweed bin Faelal, regarding his recent meeting with a rogue Pakistani General. A nuclear suitcase device is available—Russian—the price, twenty-five million American dollars—much cheaper than expected—is to be paid in oil futures and other convertible, untraceable bonds. The one stipulation—none of the payments are to be connected to American interests.

Alaweed is ecstatic. "Excellent, Akhmed, I've been planning this for twelve years." He holds out a bowl to Akhmed then rises from his mat. "The next step is to arrange delivery of the glory of my revenge to my sailing yacht."

Akhmed plucks food from a proffered silver dish with his right hand. "Yes, my old friend, that is already in process." He bows low. "May I humbly offer an opinion?"

Alaweed strokes his black, perfectly groomed beard as he nibbles absent-mindedly on a sweet cake. "What?"

Akhmed rubs his hands nervously up and down his white cotton shirt. "It is only my own lowly observation." He follows Alaweed through the flap of his plush tent into the blinding desert light. "But, what if the Infidel is watching your holdings, including your prize Swan where the scourge of the Infidel is to be delivered?"

Alaweed's black piercing eyes narrow. "What do you suggest?"

Akhmed responds, "A smaller, less ostentatious craft, one like Europeans of modest means sail with friends on ocean adventures—maybe a Beneteau—one that can carry the load but will not draw unwanted attention—one we can sail directly into the mouth of the Great Satan's largest city."

"Allah be praised for sending me such a friend as you, Akhmed. I look forward to sailing the sea with you."

"But, my great friend, I am no sailor." Akhmed is terrified. "I understood I was to make the arrangements and let more experienced brothers carry out the mission." He pauses. "Besides I would be of little use; I have a weak stomach and suffer from the malady of rolling waves."

"Nonsense, my friend," Alaweed smooths the colorful cotton layers draping his slender, elegant frame and places a soft hand on his friend's shoulder. "As my father taught me to navigate in the Mediterranean, I shall easily teach you. I would not dare to dishonor your contribution by excluding you." He leans in close to Akhmed's ear. "Don't act so modest; we are friends. I know you are secretly dying to be the one to detonate the device. It will be the pinnacle of your existence and guarantee you an unending supply of virgins."

Sickness rises in the pit of Akhmed's gut. He backs away bowing and runs around the corner of the tent and heaves his treat of palm dates and goat meat into the hot silky sands. He is not nearly so religious as his friend believes.

Alaweed smiles; he also is not nearly so religious as he preaches either. But he knows that religion is a great selling tool to promulgate his agenda of destruction and revenge. His plan has always been to let someone else have the virgins—he enjoys young boys more.

He shouts around the corner of his desert home, "I'm glad to see you are so excited, Akhmed. It shouldn't be more than a month until we see the tall buildings of our enemy. Paradise waits. Allah Akbar."

~

Back home in his workshop, Joe Human pulls the propeller blueprints from the Popular Mechanic magazine and carefully straightens them out on his workbench. He begins to study them with great eagerness.

After confirming in his own mind that the task of constructing a perfect blade for his P-51 Mustang is doable with the tools he has at his disposal, Joe begins to search through his seasoned wood blocks for the perfect grains. He turns them this way and that in his skilled hands. When he is sure he has wood that can withstand the stress, he grunts with satisfaction.

"Time to get down to business."

Not far away, up at the house, Bob and Jill are happy. Bob says to his wife, "Well, honey, that ought to keep Grandpa busy for the next couple of years."

Jill turns away from her baking and responds, "Maybe it'll keep 'im out of that archaic warplane, and folks will quit poking so much fun in our direction. Can you hand me that oven mitt, please?"

Here, be careful, don't burn yourself." Bob tugs the brim of his John Deere cap. "I don't think people make fun of Grandpa as much as they're embarrassed for him and embarrassed for themselves for being amused, but I'm betting deep down they admire his tenacity and courage to live his conviction every day."

"Here, put these on the counter." Jill pulls a cookie sheet from the oven. "You better go check on the Colonel; you don't want him to hurt himself. Some of those tools he has are pretty darn sharp."

Bob sets the cookies on the counter and grabs his denim jacket off the deer antler coat rack. "If you're good here I'll go see what our resident plane builder is up to." He turns back for a kiss. "Don't worry, he'll be fine. It'll be good for him to have a never-ending project."

They both laugh at the absurdity of the Colonel's ambition to be wheels up again.

~

The months pass, and bright spring days pass into warm, humid summer nights. The leaves on the trees lose their freshness and darken into deep, constant hues.

Joe's project has progressed steadily, and as the propeller blade takes shape he begins to feel the excitement of youth rise in his blood.

His largest problem has been to keep his finished work away from the prying eyes of his grandson. Joe may be cracked, but he's no damn fool. He knows Bob is concerned for his welfare; he also recognizes he has his nose stuck in a hole in the wall where it doesn't belong.

Joe's solution: keep a rudely carved piece of wood in sight on his busy workbench so that no one will guess at his capability or progress—he plans to buzz the barracks where he resides and the enemy stronghold in town on his maiden voyage and he wants the shock value. His finished and near-finished work is stowed under an oily canvas no one in their right mind would want to inspect for fear of getting their hands nasty.

Although Joe never ceases his work, he does occasionally slow down and glance above his bench full of sandpaper, saws, and files at a picture hanging slightly ajar on the maple-slatted barn wall. The scallop-edged black and white photo is covered by a piece of thin glass cracked diagonally, held dubiously in place by a dark, wood frame of questionable integrity.

The scene depicts a young, handsome man in uniform with his arms wrapped around a beautiful brunette. They are turned toward each other smiling, full of adoration and love. Now and again Joe will stare up at the couple and sing old standards. In between tunes he hums and talks gently to the woman, his long dead wife, Margaret, about far away

16

days and places and dreams that are yet to be and a secret rendezvous that only they know where.

Joe is busy lost in these peaceful thoughts sanding a nearly finished propeller blade, crooning a soft, raspy rendition of a Sinatra tune when Bob walks in and surprises him. "Are you coming with us tonight, Grandpa?"

Joe is startled. He turns quickly and backs against his workbench to hide his project and his embarrassment. "Go? Go where? I'm busy. Can't you see?"

Bob is patient. "Sure, Colonel, I can see you're hard at work." He shuffles forward and tries to peek over his grandfather's shoulder. "How you coming there?"

Joe bulls forward against his grandson and pushes him back. "That ain't any of your damn business, is it?"

Bob stares down in disbelief at the big dirty handprints on his clean red and blue pin striped white shirt. "Dang, Grandpa, Jill is going to skin us both alive." He studiously tries to brush the oily prints away without success and only manages to smear them worse. "She bought this shirt just for the occasion. I ain't even worn it once." He turns for the barn entrance in a huff. "Suit yourself. But if you're going to the celebration tonight you best get cleaned up and ready. I ain't waiting around for you."

"What celebration?"

"You really don't know, do you Grandpa?" He looks at his grandfather's lost expression and suddenly fells terrible. He walks over and hugs the man he has admired his entire life and in a sheepish, conciliatory voice says, "It's the Fourth, Colonel—it's the Fourth. You know, Independence Day." The nearly finished propeller blade is in full view. "Say, Grandpa, that's starting to look like something."

Joe pushes him away. "Mind your own damn business, you sneaky pup."

Bob is exasperated. "Are you going with us to watch the show or not?"

"Nope, don't like the flashing lights; and the explosions scare the devil out of me—would you too, if you had any common sense."

Bob wanders up the gravel path that leads from the barn to the house contemplating his grandfather's extraordinary life. As he enters the kitchen Jill explodes. "What happened to your shirt? Never mind, I can guess." She pulls her cotton apron off and points up the stairs. "You best get changed or we'll miss the fireworks. I take it the Colonel isn't coming?"

Bob changes the subject. "The Colonel's making real progress on that propeller."

"What? I thought you said he was making a mess. And that big mentally challenged kid, Josh, is he still hanging around?"

"I'm afraid Grandpa has been sandbagging." Bob pauses two steps up. "And yeah, yeah, Josh still visits him every couple of days or so—they're good for each other. They both live in a distorted reality."

Angry over the ruined shirt, Jill sighs. "And we don't?"

Bob ignores his wife's snide remark. "I'm a little worried. The old man's pretty crafty. What if...?" Bob's voice trails off. "What if he could make the propeller blade? But, how would he get it down the slope to the plane and install it—impossible. Besides he's still not done with the first one." Bob continues his ascent. "Yeah, he couldn't possibly be strong enough to lift the pieces into place—probably won't live that long anyway."

Down in the workshop Joe is dancing a jig. The propeller blade his grandson saw isn't the first; it's the fourth and final one. He winks at the girl in the picture. "Won't be long now, Margaret; I'm coming to get you. Heaven ain't too high to keep you from me. We're going to go flying—just the two of us."

~

Akhmed has been hanging on the gunnels feeding the Yellow Tail green bile for two days. He prays he will die soon. While he and Alaweed had sailed close to the rocky outcrops in the Mediterranean he had begun to feel confident in his new skills of navigation and sailing. But as soon as they had entered the Atlantic, the waves had risen in ever increasing swells and the sickening dizziness had begun. The rail had been his constant companion ever since.

Alaweed can hardly contain his delight at his friend's discomfort. "Can I get you something good to eat my friend—something to settle your stomach—perhaps the blood of a kid?" He laughs quietly as his offer sets off another round of dry heaves. "Or perhaps the..."

Akhmed gasps, "Please, brother, the only help for me is death. If you love me, kill me quickly. My suffering is great." Alaweed's smugness is lost on him.

Alaweed places his hands on his hips, leans back and laughs loudly and answers, "That I cannot do my loyal friend." His mind races ahead. "Yes, but if I did kill him very slowly—perhaps sawed his green face off with a dull knife—that would even more pleasurable than watching his present distress.

"But no, I will need his strength to place and arm the two hundred-pound, eight kiloton device. Perhaps he can wear the backpack it is contained in. Imagine when it detonates—body parts flying into oblivion." He shudders. "What pleasure!"

A boat on the horizon approaches fast and breaks Alaweed's musing. He is instantly on the alert. He lifts his binoculars and brings

19

the fast-approaching craft into sight. He expects to be found out and boarded at any moment. He is needlessly worried. The other captain lifts a bottle of scotch in salute as the four, three hundred horsepower mercruisers speed by carrying a boatload of half-naked women. "Infidel dogs, sons of the Great Satan." He spits over the side.

Akhmed once again occupies his attention. "Stop that heaving, there is work to be done." He has no pity. "I should have brought a young boy; at least he would have kept me entertained." He turns away in disgust.

"Come on, Josh, you can do it—we've got to do it." Joe is grunting and straining and encouraging Josh with every ounce of grit he has left in his worn-out body to lift the propeller into place. He had known this day would come and had waited patiently for summer to end—that moment when Jill and Bob would leave him alone for the afternoon while they attended the annual Labor Day church picnic up at the lake.

He had feigned weakness and got them to ask Josh's folks if the boy could visit and sit with him for the day. So far, the plan had worked to perfection, and if Josh could just steady the propeller housing for a moment more the first phase of his mission to fly again would be accomplished.

Joe laughs and says to Josh, "That a boy, hold her right there. I've got the bolt started." He grabs in the back pocket of his mechanic's coverall for his half inch drive ratchet. He pulls it out and, in a few seconds, has the main bolt secured. "You can let go now, Josh. I think we've done it."

Josh puts his massive arms down, looks at Joe and says, "Can we get some chocolate cake now? I'm hungry."

Joe smiles at the innocent boy. If there is anyone in the vicinity more deserving than Josh, he hasn't met them yet. "Just a second, let me tighten these other bolts, and I'll take you up to the barracks for a treat."

Josh stamps his foot. "But, I want some now. You promised me."

"You know where the kitchen is, don't you, Josh? Go on up and help yourself. The door is unlocked and the cake's on the counter. I'll be there directly." He hates to lie to Josh, but under the circumstances it's best if Josh isn't a part of what happens next. He wouldn't understand. "Go on, now." Joe shoos the boy away. "I'll be right up." He watches Josh trudge toward the house and looks skyward. "Yes sir, with any luck I'll be up yonder in the next few minutes."

Joe slaps at his jacket pocket--empty. "Whew, for a minute I thought I forgot to leave the note." He hollers after Josh, "And don't fool with that envelope on the table."

~

Three weeks at sea has much improved Akhmed's health and confidence. "What is the date, Alaweed?"

"September 2nd, only nine days more until the Infidel Beast memorializes our greatest victory." He can barely contain his disdain. "After this September there will be nowhere for them to gather, only a pile of radioactive ash to remind the Great Satan that Mohammed is the greatest prophet and that Allah alone reigns supreme."

Akhmed nods his assent. "Victory will be ours. We are less than a hundred miles from the city. When do we arm the device?"

Alaweed grins. "Funny you should ask this question today Akhmed; we will make the device live after morning prayers. Our time has come, Allah be praised."

"I have saved our ceremonial prayer rugs for this occasion." Akhmed is excited. "The Imam himself consecrated them. Surely God is Great, and we shall prevail."

Alaweed is pleased. "Go below and make certain the rugs are clean and flawless. Allah will witness our finest prayers and blessings."

Ahkmed complies. "It is as you say." He backs away bowing in his humility.

~

After his regular pre-flight check, Joe climbs into the cockpit. The moment of truth is at hand. His bird hasn't been off the ground in thirty years. He hits the switch as she sputters once and fires. The spinning blade swirls the air. He hasn't felt propeller blowback for a long time. He's missed it.

Joe knows he's cracked, and he remembers how he was cracked—the tracers from the sights of an enemy gunner had found him and then, the two blows that had widened the crack—the news of his son, J.D., shot down over the jungles of Vietnam and the wreath he had placed on the casket of his beloved Margaret soon after.

Joe has never pretended to fly as everyone thinks—he's never been that cracked. He's fooled them all with that ploy. He only needed a safe place to be alone with his life—to reminisce—to feel and wonder why last memories present a sharper image than first memories and all the other times in between.

He releases the brake and taxis down the hill; rolls out into the flat valley and without hesitation hits the throttle. The bird jumps forward and accelerates down the grass airstrip eager to be airborne. Once wheels up, Joe buzzes the town and barracks for fun and then heads out to sea and leaves the ground clutter behind.

~

"**S**omething's not right." Jill is staring out of the Subaru Outback's windshield.

Bob is nonchalant—figures he's in for another relationship quiz. "What do you mean?"

"I can't put my finger on it, honey, but something is different."

Bob turns toward his wife in consternation. "Come on, dear, we go up and down, what, four five times a week; nothing ever changes between us except the seasons."

Jill is insistent. "I don't mean us." She leans over toward the driver's side, braces herself on the console and puts the other hand on her husband's forearm. "Oh, my God, Oh, my God, Oh, my God; it can't be!"

Bob slams on the brakes. "What in the hell is wrong with you?"

Jill is speechless for a brief moment. When she finds her voice it's the voice of someone who's seen a miracle or been a part of a horrendous act of violence, but still can't believe it's happening to them. "It's gone—vanished."

"What's gone?" Bob is exasperated. He's staring out of the window in the direction Jill is pointing and sees nothing—nothing but rocky hillside. "I don't see a thing. You must be...holy shit, I don't see anything. Oh, my God! I don't see anything. Grandpa's plane is gone. H-o-l-y shit!"

He stomps on the gas pedal and throws gravel out from under the rear tires and skids sideways on the mountain road.

Jill screams, "God bless it, Bob. Be careful; you're going to kill us too!"

The words sink in as Bob regains control of the small SUV. "Kill us too—you don't think Grandpa is...?" The thought is too horrible to utter. "Let's get on up to the house so we can get a better look at the valley."

Jill adds, "I call 911."

Bob punches the gas again.

~

Alaweed bin Faelal has backed the jib and turned the rudder so their forty-one-foot Beneteau will remain in irons with the stern facing east until prayers are over. Akhmed has unrolled their prayer rugs and is already in process of kneeling to face Mecca when they hear the first faint buzz of an airplane approaching. He shields his eyes for a good view. "It is nothing, Alaweed, only a weekend aviator out sightseeing—nothing to concern us."

Alaweed, already jittery because of the approaching deadline, is not as sure. His plan is to survive this mission—not get caught up in mistakes and emotion. "Perhaps, Akhmed, you are correct. But let us be certain." He pulls his long-range glasses for a closer look. With a relieved sigh he returns the binoculars to their case. "You were right, my friend, it's an old vintage WWII airplane. My father had an aviator enthusiast friend who owned one like it—I remember it as a boy. It is no threat to us."

Akhmed is reassured. "Shall we commence with our prayers?"

"Yes, Allah Akbar." Alaweed falls to his knees. "He will protect us."

As Joe Human approaches the sailing craft, the hairs on the nape of his neck rise, he decides that perhaps he should get a better look—perhaps someone is in distress. He rolls gently, eases on the stick, and slowly circles the craft. His plan is to offer assistance if needed.

24

Two men in robes rise from prone positions on the deck.

"What do you think that cowardly dog wants?" Akhmed asks Alaweed. "Do you think he will report our presence to the authorities?"

Alaweed waves at the plane to reassure the pilot all is well. "There is no reason to believe that. Look how low he flies, he's an old man with white hair; the only harm he could cause to us is if he were unlucky enough to crash into us."

Akhmed shudders. "The bomb is armed, brother. That would kill us all."

Joe decides to circle in even closer for no particular reason other than he wants a better look at the boat. He likes the hull design.

This move, along with Akhmed's warning that they are on a boat with an armed eight hundred kiloton device, panics Alaweed. He begins to wave his arms wildly and shake his fist and shout at the pilot. "Get away from us you mangy, wrinkled, old dog." To reinforce his message, he pulls an AR15 with a banana clip from a hidden compartment below the helm and fires warning shots into the crystal sky.

Joe is puzzled by this action. Then the cracked part of him is in another time and dimension and angry and scared and fighting for his life. He's not pretending anymore. The blood coursing through his veins is real. The bullets are real. The enemy is real. He pulls up hard, banks sharply right and to the horror of the two Arab men he dives straight for their boat.

Alaweed begins to fire in earnest directly at the approaching P-51. He shouts loudly to a cowering Akhmed. "Get up you cowardly leavings of a goat. Grab the other rifle and help."

Joe has the sailboat lined up in his sights. He squeezes the trigger. Nothing happens. His guns have no ammo. It dawns on him; they were never loaded—he'd forgotten that part. He yanks the stick hard into his gut and banks hard. When he looks back both men are still firing at him.

"Will he come again?" Akhmed screams at Alaweed.

"How do I know what that son of a motherless she-camel will do? I only know we are too close to success to be ruined by one old man."

As Joe comes in fast a second time both men realize simultaneously that he is not firing back. Alaweed laughs out loud. "He has no weapons, Akhmed; he is only trying to taunt us. Two can play that game."

Akhmed asks his friend, "So what is our plan now?"

"We'll shoot the dirty dog dung from the sky." Alaweed is still reveling in the knowledge that his adversary has no weapons with which to return fire. He aims his rifle in the direction of Joe's fading Mustang and says to Akhmed, "Come brother, let us stand together and send this Infidel into the blast furnace of hell."

Akhmed, enthused by Alaweed, joins him on the stern.

Joe climbs slowly into the sun and circles lazily out of range—breathing in his moment with exhilaration. When he is ready and assured of what must be done, he rolls and begins a third dive at the boat. This time his angle of descent is steep—very steep—too steep.

The misbegotten sons of the desert are chanting Allah Akbar and laying down a withering hail of bullets at the approaching Angel of Death.

Joe Human wears a smile on his rugged face, the wind is blowing through his thick, white hair, and the sun is at his back. He is chanting too. "Soon, Margaret, soon—yes, soon, soon, soon—I'll be there soon."

~

Once they reach the house, Jill rushes for the phone in the kitchen—their cell service is non-existent. Bob is right on her heels. As she places the emergency call she sees Bob lift an envelope from the table and open it. She shrugs her shoulders in a question?

Bob pulls a letter from inside the unsealed packet and begins to silently read. He waves at Jill. "It's from Grandpa. Hang up."

"What?"

"Hang up; they can't help us...or him."

"What?" Jill walks over slowly and places her hands on her husband's shoulders. She says quietly, "Read it to me, please."

Bob clears his throat and begins: "My dear children, what is there to say? Goodbye—so long—see you in the funny papers? I will not be back. Don't stress. Don't shed tears. It's just that it's time—time for my one last great adventure. I'm not sure exactly what and where that is yet, but by God I'm sure I'm going to fly there—wherever there is.

"So, here's all I got to say: If we—you and me—don't follow our one true heart what is life? How do we connect to the natural order of perfection if we don't possess a true heart—a heart full of truth; that's the closest to God we can hope to achieve as mortal beings.

"I know you two think I'm cracked—and I may be but remember this: in the end we're all going to lose everything we ever knew anyway. So why not live every day, before every day becomes yet another day of waiting to die—of dreading the inevitable.

"I've decided it's time for me to accept my mortality and embrace death with fervor. In the end I pray I leave the world better than I found it—that I go in love with life—gasping to suck down every last drop of oxygen available. All my leftover air I bequeath to you. Use it wisely!"

Tears stain Bob's face. He stands and takes his wife by the hand, "Come on, let's walk. I don't know where Grandpa has gone, but I'd sure like to see where he launched from. A short time later they stare in disbelief at the spot where the Mustang was recently released from its tethered captivity.

Far in the distance, out to sea, a mushroom cloud expands into the heavens.

Jill shudders at the sight and points. "You think Grandpa is connected to that?"

Bob pulls his wife close and says, "Who else? That Joe Human sure had some guts."

The Circle

Scrunched down on one knee, ready to shoot, Shocklett Onile Sneed stares at the circle with a focus bordering intensity. Ever-lengthening shadows dance in the Florida sun.

The palm of her hand rests tight against the taw line. A sharp turn and a twist of the thumb and forefinger and the shooter, a rust colored cat's eye bolts across the smoothed earth at the perfect height and angle and strikes the target—a clear agate. It sails from the ring.

Shocklett's cat's eye sits down in the sand, spinning in its own singular orbit. In unison five sandy-haired boys squatted around the drawn circle on the ground cry out in dismay and astonishment. Shocklett has won for the fifth time in a row.

~

At that exact moment a new shadow loomed eerily across the circle causing a sharp, prolonged, intake of breath from the players. A hairy, calloused hand gripped my arm, and none too gently helped me to my feet. My right foot tippy-toed the ground while my left foot waved goodbye or hello or good Lord I'm about to fly away and never be heard from again. Either way I was in trouble.

The lean-muscled vice holding my arm refused to relent in response to my squirmy protests. A gruff voice said, "Ya hear yore momma calling you, Dakotah Johnson? It's supper time. I'm hungry an' the rest of the fam'ly is all waitin' on you ta eat. What'd I tell ya 'bout not comin' home right quick when yore momma calls? I know ya heared her. Well, did ya or not?"

In a little voice, I mumbled back, "Yes, sir. I heared 'er."

Daddy gripped my arm tighter and gave me a little shake. "Speak up, I cain't hear you, Dakotah. Did you hear yore Momma callin' for ya or not?"

This time I managed a braver, surer answer. After all, Daddy couldn't eat me, could he?" Yes, sir. I heard Momma calling me. But, I thought…" My excuse gets lost in Daddy's stern stare. Maybe, he could eat me. Time to shut up.

The other kids backed off a considerable distance, the game of marbles forgotten for the time being. They discussed my fate, in smothered whispers, until I heard, over Daddy's rumbling, an ever-growing sound of snickers quickly working their way up toward outright, unabashed laughter at the calamity that had befallen me. They all knew Daddy.

"All right then, tell these here childr'n what I promised ya the nex' time ya ignored yore momma's yoo-hoo an' didn't come when ya was supposed to. Go on, tell 'em. I want 'em ta hear from, yore own two lips, so's they'll all know yore daddy keeps his promises."

"You said I's gonna get whupped all the way home next time Momma had to ask you to come and get me."

"Do ya know how worried yore momma gets when ya stay out and do ya have any idée how much she nags at me ta straighten ya out?" Before I could form a response, Daddy patted his middle, "But, don't ya worry, son, I got the right medicine. A good dose of Dr. Black will cure what ails ya. "'Fore I'm done with, ya you'll wish you'd listened better. Yore a might hard-headed, but I got the answer to yore momma's unease." Daddy tapped his belt again, "I'm tired of hearin' her fuss. Do you hear me, Dakotah Johnson?"

Through the chastised taste of snot and tears on the back of my denim sleeve I answered meekly, "Yes, sir. I surely do wish I'd listened to Momma."

Boy, do I wish I'd listened to Momma. Daddy's strop is gonna hurt for sure. I'm too big for a whuppin' like this in front of my friends. I ain't never gonna live this down. I hope Daddy don't hit too hard or miss and hit me with that big flat buckle. Oh, my Lord. Everybody 'll be talking about me for months at school. What'll I say? I hope I don't cry too much. I'll punch the first boy that says anything. I will. What about the girls? Oh, who cares about them, anyway?

Daddy snaked his leather belt through the wide loops on his khaki britches. The strop, two inches wide, looked six. He took me by the elbow and pointed. "Well then, let's get started. One monkey don't make the whole show. Dark is closin' in and I ain't plannin' to let no pesky mosquiters suck my blood this evenin'."

That sand-rutted road home provided a long, uphill lesson, but the toughest part of my walk-hop-run wasn't Daddy's broad, black belt. The toughest part was the relentless marble mob that whooped and hollered and poked fun from a safe distance at my expense every time the leather burned my bottom, and Daddy…for all his talk…turned out to be in no hurry to get to the supper table.

The Dream

The red L.C.D. flashes 2:21 anxiety as I bolt upright in bed, drenched in cold sweat. My lungs heave and my mind races as I try to suck down one good breath and collect my thoughts. At fifty, everything's gone; job, house, cars, wife; even Brewer, my onetime loyal Lab. Blame the Great Recession! It's just a matter of time until the bank moves me out.

However, as intense as the rest of my life is, the dream that has awakened me out of a sound sleep every night for the last week is about something altogether different. It's the same dream I dreamed at seventeen, Blue Steel Spirit, the band I co-founded in 1975. We were good man, I mean, really good and headed straight for the top until our lead guitar player, Fast Denny, fell in love, decided to get hitched and bailed on the band. I was so sure we were about to hit it big back then, I wonder... maybe my recurring dream is a sign. Maybe it is time to try, again. Maybe with a little luck we could pull it off? Maybe...

Early, the next morning, my first call is to Fast Denny, who is now Mr. V.P. in charge of harvesting for a large, cooperate agricultural firm. The conversation is nice; too nice. We haven't spoken in a while and it's cool to reminisce over all the good times we shared, but in the end, he simply laughs off the idea of re-forming the band as a crazy left-over sophomoric dream and completely unrealistic.

He has his feet firmly on the ground with a pension and retirement planning in the works and he's not about to risk any of that on my, what did he call it? Oh yeah! He called it the half-baked-too-long-in the-sun, dissonant notion of an over-the-hill-wannabe who still had his head in the clouds and never found the time or interest to grow up. Well, at least he still likes me.

"Hey, listen Kid, I'm sorry, I've gotta run, my secretary is hounding me, I've got two, really important calls waiting. Stay in touch. Oh…and Kid, if there's anything I can do to help…"

"Thanks, Fast Denny, I appreciate it, but I'll be alright. Give my best to the wife."

"Sure, let's talk again soon. Stay in touch, Kid."

"Yeah, okay, take it easy, Denny."

What a letdown, but that's okay, lead guitar players are a dime a dozen. It's a bass player I need. So, three days later, Cliff and I meet and reminisce over more good times…etc… etc… etc. Same result. Bass players are easy to find too.

My old friends have moved on. They can both take it easy. My blues muse takes over for a moment: I wonder about dreams tucked away / in remote corners of our head / forlorn notes covered in dust no light of day / do those cobwebs ever draw breath?

Dang it! Now what? It's Saturday morning and I insist on my quiet time on weekend mornings. I have a ten o'clock rule, everybody that knows me knows that, no phone calls and no racket allowed before ten. What the…? Oh shoot! It registers. It's the lawn service. I forgot to cancel. I can't afford to pay them anymore, so there's nothing to do except face the music.

I gather myself and walk outside to tell the foreman, Shane, so he can pass the word onto his boss. Shane is a tall, slender, polite, young man, with long hair; kinda reminds me of myself a hundred years ago.

Coffee cup in hand, we have the conversation. I can tell he is disappointed to lose the work, but he says, "No worries, this day job is only meant to fill up the in-betweens until my band gets its big break. Music is my real occupation and a honey-colored Strat is, without question, the love of my life. We've worked really hard to be ready when the major labels come calling…and they will, believe me.

I have to be honest with you though, I'm startin' to be more than a little worried our drummer might bail at the exact moment we're about to blow up. Man, he's a monster and he'll be hard to replace. Maybe he'll stay, but the girl he plans to marry next week doesn't have much soul. I hope I'm wrong, but I'm afraid she's already got her mind made up to drive a wedge between him and the other band members. She is definitely the jealous type. I don't know what we'll do if… I'm sure you know the old story Mr. Robinson, it's time to settle down and get a real job and you've got a family to support now…you understand, don't you?"

"Yeah, well…as a matter of fact, I know exactly what you're coming from! I've already seen that movie and I promise you it did not have a happy ending."

A vague thought fleets through my mind and my heart skips a beat. I wonder…? "You know it's kinda funny we're having this conversation, Shane, because, as strange as it sounds, I've been trying to get my old band back together this week, without much success. We were pretty good back in the day, and I thought it might be fun to hang out and play a little music to see if any of the magic still exists, but it seems they're too busy these days to give any credence to the dream."

He laughs quietly, with barely concealed skepticism, the way only a very confident young man can, "So you're a musician? I had no idea. What do you play?"

"Oh, I'm not a musician, I'm only a drummer." It's every guitar player's joke, so he laughs again, but this time it's an appreciative laugh of shared experience.

"Hey, Shane, I have some originals on tape, would you like to give 'em a listen?"

He humors me and says "Sure man, why not that would be great. I love OLD music."

"Great, hang on a sec and I'll grab you a copy."

Three weeks go by, and I have so many other matters closing in me from all sides that I have completely forgotten my conversation with Shane and then out of the blue, he rings me up.

"Hey, listen, Mr. Robinson, I wanted to let you know, me and the boys think you had a pretty good sound goin' back in the day."

He actually listened to the tapes? I'm shocked. I figured he was humoring an old man and the nearest trashcan he passed had probably gotten a tape worm.

"Thanks, I appreciate that, Shane…and by the way, my friends call me Kid."

"Anyway, the thing is, Mr.…umm, I... I mean…Kid, I wonder if I could ask you a big favor, our drummer has…how can I put this nicely, abandoned us at his wife's request and we need someone to sit in for rehearsals. Would you be interested in playing a few practice sessions until we can find a permanent replacement?

We're kinda under the gun. Our promo gig at Universal studios is coming up in a few weeks and it's really important for the band to be tight. A lot of producers are gonna be out in the audience that night. It's the chance of a lifetime for us and we'd hate to be late for the Show."

Breathe, Kid! Breathe! "Yeah, sure, right on, I'd be happy to help out. What time and where?"

Turns out, Shane's band is every bit as good as he said they were and lucky me, I find myself playing the Universal gig with them. The critics love us, and the papers are full of rave reviews the next day. It also turns out; one of the producers looking for new talent at the show is the friend of a friend of a friend. That seals my fate. Funny how old saws about a small world and coincidental meetings get to be old saws; they're true.

The red L.C.D. flashes 2:21 anxiety, again! Bolt upright in bed! Cold Sweat! Same dream! C'mon try to suck down one good breath. Get your head together. Okay? Okay. Okay. I roll over, wipe the beads of sweat from my forehead, with the back of my hand, pull the curtains apart on the oval, tour bus, window and stare for a long time in disbelief at the lighted street scene.

In the last year we've had three tunes in the top ten and our last song is still sitting at the top of the charts. It's been quite a ride. So, gimme a break, this may be the last stop on a twelve-month world tour, but I'm still nervous, the gig tomorrow night is as cool as it gets.

We've officially arrived. Sleep, fog and a tinted window are all that remain between me and the ginger brick on the building: Carnegie Hall.

Jake's Exhilaration

Jake had always been wilder than hell. Everybody knew it. They all said he was gonna wind up sporting a striped suit on a chain gang or upside down in a ditch with a blade between his shoulders, bleeding out all over the world.

From the time he was a small boy with big, flashing blue eyes and a smile that refused to be ignored, everyone who came into his orbit immediately became a part of the madness and charisma Jake toted in his hip pocket with an easy, reckless charm.

That was his secret, he made everybody feel alive. His enthusiasm filled every pore of everybody with his contagious non-stop zest for drawing air in and out: deep and clean ever expanding and ever refreshing. When he was around you knew why you were alive and how to be alive and what was possible and that nothing was impossible and that you were going to be strong and vibrant and full of living forever.

He was the boy every mother warned her daughter about and every father was afraid his daughter would love with abandon and everyone, young and old, wanted to be, but were scared to be or knew in their hearts they could never be.

They were intrigued and repulsed. They wanted him. They needed him. But in the end, he frightened them too much. He already knew what they hated to admit; ultimately, they'd judge him harshly.

But this morning, Jake was just another seventeen-year-old kid trying to find a light in the darkness that enveloped his world. He had acquired the keys to his best friend's powder-blue, four-on-the-floor, '69 GT Mustang through cajole, deceit and outright begging.

It didn't matter to him how he'd got the keys. He'd got them. He'd got them now and they were jingling in his right hand while his mind turned left hand circles figuring out how to make the most of a sunny Saturday morning in a fast-ass car.

Jake had already acquired a reputation for a heavy foot, so as he sidled out of the front screen door and let it slam shut, Lonnie made him promise the speedometer would never read over sixty and the tach would never swing past 2700rpm; well below the 5000rpm redline.

In fact, Lonnie made him promise twice. He did and Jake lied both times, knowingly and willingly, lied for the hell of it, lied because he could and lied because telling the truth bored the hell out of him.

Lonnie shrugged. Jake smiled. Said he needed a Goody Powder for the headache he felt coming on and needed to make a run to the lonesome little store that sat deftly at the crossroads two miles away to get it.

It was a lame excuse, but Lonnie knew the road there and back was defended by five thousand acres of empty farm land, so he let Jake have his wheels. How much trouble could one boy collect that quickly? Jake was about to tip his hand—it would be no trouble at all.

DeeDee was on Jake's mind too. Talk about one fine piece of ass, he thought to himself as eased out onto the two-lane, sectioned concrete pavement in the opposite direction of the store. Man, this is my chance to score with that little girl. She's working just over the county line in the family nursery with her brother, Marion. I'll bet she'll be happy to escape the drudgery and fill my passenger seat with nothing more than a wink and a nod and who knows, with a little sweet talk, maybe the backseat too.

~

"**D**ang it!" DeeDee inspected her ruined nails as she wiped the dirty sweat from her forehead and kept digging in the pearlite-filled peat bed. No boy is ever going to look my way twice as long as Daddy keeps me cooped up in this dingy, plastic-covered hellhole. If she had to cut and stick one more piece of philly stock in the rich black earth today she was going to scream. Yuck! She wanted to be anywhere, but here. Where was her knight in shining armor?

~

Clothed in black vinyl and Detroit metal, Jake hummed the new Three Dog Night tune, "One Is the Loneliest Number", while he fumbled around with his right hand for the unfamiliar location of the car lighter. The front windows were rolled down and his long unruly blonde hair whipped his lean, chiseled features unmercifully. He didn't care. Hell, he enjoyed the wild feeling it fed in him—in fact, he embraced it.

Finally, the lighter button popped, and he stuck the red-hot glow solidly on the end of the Winston Red dangling from his top lip and took a long-satisfied drag. The kind of smug, I've-got-the-world-by-the-tail-drag only an immortal teenager certain he'll never grow old can pull. He didn't give a damn at that moment about anything, but the exhilaration of being young.

~

"**J**acob come here you little pig-headed brat. What have you gotten yourself mixed up with now? How many times do I have to tell you to do your chores? Just 'cause it's a Saturday and you ain't got no school don't mean you're off the hook. If your daddy comes home for dinner and you ain't finished cleaning that tractor barn before he gets washed up for dinner you know what you're gonna be in for. You do know, right?

My God, how can one ten-year-old boy make such a mess without accomplishing nothin'. The way you act you ain't never gonna amount to a hill of beans. You're grandpa would be so disappointed! All right come here. I didn't mean to make you cry, but you gotta learn there's rules here and life is hard. I'm just trying to look out for you. You don't want that big leather strop of your daddy's to add to your misery, do you? It's all right, come on over here, dry your eyes on my apron and give me a hug around the neck. That's it. You look better already. Now get on down there and finish cleaning them stalls before your daddy tans both our hides."

"Yes, Ma'am."

~

The Y in the road came up fast. It always did, on the Laughlin curve, at eighty-five miles an hour. Jake hit the brakes hard, downshifted even harder, slung the steering wheel to the right, hand over hand, in a hard arc and skidded sideways through the turn. He reveled in the deep gurgle of the resonator as he poured the coal to the Holley four barrel. The little pony responded to his gruff maneuver and leapt out on to worn, narrow asphalt leaving a streak of burned rubber and wasted effort.

~

"Come on DeeDee it's break time." Marion offered. "How about holler out back to them boys we got loadin' peat tubs and see if they want something from the store. You know what, never mind, it's Saturday. Go ahead and ask them sorry-asses if they wanna ride along in the back of the truck."

40

Daddy wouldn't think about letting 'em on the truck except to pick 'em up or drop, 'em off, he thought to himself, but he ain't here and I'm in charge so I'm gonna make the call. They ain't gonna hit a lick at a snake while I'm gone anyway. Might as well keep 'em where I can see 'em. At least that a way I'll know what their up to.

~

The little Mustang whirled along as Jake wound the rpm's tighter and tighter and speed shifted into fourth without ever touching the clutch. At a hundred and ten the light poles got closer and closer together and the bumps in the road grew bigger by the second.

Jake only had one hand on the wheel—actually he had no hands on the wheel, only his left wrist bent over the top of the wheel in the most casual carefree pose he could muster. He was driving and smoking and listening to The Stones on the radio now and daydreaming about what it would be like to bend DeeDee over the long hood of the GT.

He wondered if she was still a virgin and whether or not she would wriggle and scream—shit! He nearly lost control as the right front tire lost the pavement and pitched the car with a thud into a bumpy sideways slide. Jake gripped the wheel hard with both hands, took his foot off the gas pedal and slowed enough so he could nudge the trembling treads back on to the road.

Man, was he lucky he wasn't upside down. He skidded to a stop, caught his breath— "you cain't always get what you want..." and thought to himself, I'd better pay closer attention, if I wreck his car Lonnie is gonna beat my ass. Damn!

~

"Daddy I swear to God…"

"What'd you jus' say Jacob? You swear to who?"

"I'm sorry, I'm sorry I want cuss again, Daddy. I swear to…I promise …Pleeaase, I'll do what you say next time. I'm sorry, I'm sorry, I'm sorry. Pleeaasse don't whip me no more. I'll get this barn cleaner than you could ever imagine. Pleeaasse give me one more chance. Owwy, Owwy, Owwy. Pleeaasse Daddy don't hit me no more, I'll do what you say."

"Okay, boy, go on in and git washed up for dinner and wipe them sissy tears outta your eyes. You're getting' too big to squall and carry on that way over a little whuppin'. You'll embarrass yourself in front of your momma and the other young'uns."

"Yes, sir"

"Alright then, git!"

I wiped the tears away on the back of my dirt-streaked hands as I headed up to the house and managed a good smudge on my face so I'd get the question from Momma and without me saying a word, Daddy would catch the devil for giving me what I so richly deserved.

I was a hell of a lot more mischievous than Momma ever thought and as time went on some folks called me downright dangerous. I think they might've got a little carried away with that description, but that's their business.

Besides, that wasn't for several years to come and they got most of that description off the local six o'clock news; that damn lady reporter really raked me over the coals; over nothing. I had no idea spinning donuts in the local magistrate's front yard would cause such a stir.

42

Maybe if I hadn't brought his daughter home ten minutes late and maybe if I hadn't been a gentleman and walked her inside to explain and maybe if my shirt hadn't been on wrong side out and backwards, he wouldn't have been so narrow minded and went for my throat and maybe I wouldn't have been in such an all fired hurry to leave the premises and maybe his precious lawn wouldn't have had so many skid marks wandering around on it.

~

The aged Chevy truck the Carlton nursery used for hauling plants wore a dull, faded, green coat and the loose tappets hidden under the leaky, oil-soaked valve cover, clacked steadily as the pistons fired more or less in unison and only back-fired on occasion. It wasn't exactly a fine-tuned machine—in fact it sounded more like a Sears's sewing machine than a Chevrolet, but it served its weekly chore of hauling cardboard boxes filled with three-inch potted Philodendron back and forth to the train depot.

Marion made sure everybody was loaded on their rickety ride and cautioned 'em twice to sit down and get out of the way as he adjusted the rearview mirror. Then, he backed up and turned around on the sandspurs and sawdust in front of the slatted shade house and eased up the rutted path that connected the nursery to the main road.

He came to a rolling stop at the junction, looked both ways, let out on the clutch slowly and then, as luck would have it, a bad pressure plate caused the engine to shudder, sputter and die and brought them to full stop, leaving the bent nose of the grille hanging out over the ragged edge of the asphalt.

~

Even though he had been to the location on several occasions, Jake had never learned to judge the gaping hole in the tall weeds alongside the road where the nursery opened onto the pavement. He knew when you crossed the tracks it came up fast, but this morning he was feeling so free and alive that what should've been the first thing on his mind wasn't on his mind at all.

He was still bending DeDee over the hood when the click clack of the railroad tracks sitting on an uneven, creosote pine bed passed underneath the car and he realized that he was going to blow by the opening at a hundred plus miles an hour. Suddenly, a green metallic glint slid into his right peripheral vision. Instinctively, he swerved.

~

Daddy looked around the barn and thought to himself, I don't have no idée what Mom and I are gonna do with that boy. His heart is good, but something feral is growing inside him. He shook his head and started an overwhelmed, tired trudge uphill to the dinner table. Sometimes Jacob was too much to handle, even for a tough Cracker like him.

By the time Daddy got to the conch peas and cornbread, the conversation had already headed somewhere else. Thank goodness. It seems business was picking up and gas and interest cost might be easing up and

"Jacob, I'm sorry if you think I was a little hard on ya earlier, but boy you have got to learn some responsibility and how to finish what you start. I tell ya what; I'll make you a deal, do a good job and finish cleaning out that ol' barn, then do a little extra for me, polish that Model A, hot rod I been workin' on and I'll teach ya to drive."

Momma gave him a look that would have shriveled a dried prune. "You cain't be serious. Teaching a boy that age to drive a car like that is asking for trouble. What can you be thinking. Jacob go on and finish your chores, me and your Daddy have something to discuss. I said git! And don't you dare go near that deathtrap your daddy's building. I said git, Jacob. Go on now and you better listen to what I say if you know what's good for you."

Daddy caught hell, but his T-Bucket was polished to a fine sheen and for all his barking and growling, he kept his word. I learned to drive, first in the fields, then on red clay roads and finally, by age thirteen I was pretty much running the local law insane with my lead-foot antics.

~

Jake yanked the steering wheel hard left, slammed in the clutch and stood on the brakes with a booted foot, but it was way too little too late. Out of control the coupe went into yet another tailspin—which quickly became a backward driving adventure.

But Jake stayed cool and sure of himself. He downshifted, steered with perfect touch and let the new Michelin tires smoke their life away as he headed the backslid Mustang the other direction. He came to a screeching halt on the road in front of the 1953 pickup filled with cheering kids, who wanted to see him do it all over again.

If the clutch on the old half-ton had visited the shop when it was supposed to, it wouldn't have caused the truck to stall when it did and there would have been a thousand pieces of mangled flesh and metal melded together all over God's green earth.

Hell, those kids had no clue how close they'd come to an unexpected visit to St. Peter at the Pearly Gates. It never crossed their minds. Jake had them too exhilarated with his wild stunt. Their whole morning took new meaning.

DeeDee smiled a big crooked, white smile and looked straight at him and flirted and he grinned right back, but it was her next move that really made him smile. She slid out of the creaky passenger door, sashayed over and leaned her elbows on the top of his open window.

He nodded his head toward the empty bucket seat beside him. "Git in, DeeDee, I'll take you anywhere you wanna go."

He didn't need to ask twice because, as he would soon learn, her imagination was better than his. DeDee climbed in through the tapered passenger window onto the front seat head-over-heels and they roared away with blue-black tire smoke and her brother's protests hanging onto the hot July morning.

By the time Jake showed up in the Mustang later that afternoon, poor Lonnie had heard the story over and over from at least five well-meaning friends. In fact, he had heard five different versions over and over, each more embellished than the last and from those stories he knew two things for sure: he had the hottest car in the county, and he was gonna rip Jake's head off when he got his hands on 'im.

Jake should've been upset by all this noise coming from his friends and roommate, but instead he smiled a quiet self-satisfied smile because he understood why they were upset. They all wanted to be him and loved him, and he was only seventeen and laughing and full of himself and he knew two true things: knew them for certain; it was Saturday and DeeDee was definitely no virgin.

The Treasure Divers

Mallory and longtime dive partner, Johnson, have been working an active treasure site along the Florida coastline very day for the past three months. Their monotonous job is to pull a magnetometer towfish attached to a C-cable behind a twenty-foot Carolina Skiff armed with a 200 horsepower Yamaha outboard back and forth in steady swing patterns looking for anomalies in the readings—anomalies that could indicate the heavy metal all treasure hunters dream about—gold.

Mallory, bored by the consistent wave action and constant silence of Johnson abruptly turns his tall, lean frame away from the helm for a moment, shades his dark green eyes against the July glare and jibes at his partner. "Are you sure that thing is turned on? I haven't heard a beep in the last half hour."

Johnson's only reply is a loud, obnoxious burp. He spits over the side and sullenly ignores Mallory. He's a quiet man by nature. Not much escapes his craggy red-bearded mouth unless he's got something important to say or unless he's mad at Mallory—neither is true at the moment and he refuses to be drawn into Mallory's discontent.

The fish attached to the magnetometer and trolled behind the boat by fifty-foot lead lines is designed to detect differences in the earth's magnetic field as it passes over metal objects. Johnson's task is to monitor the anomalies and enter the way points (latitude and longitude) in the computer of any metal detected on or under the ocean floor. Every time the hand on the "mag" pegs a prescient chill of treasure to come runs up his spine.

47

Mallory follows the track of their boat on a computer screen, maintains a relatively straight line and make fifty-foot turn-outs every half-mile as they run back and forth. They'll come back and dive the GPS coordinates later. That's the fun part—usually. A daydream if ever there was one.

So far, all the erstwhile treasure hunters have to show for their summer of hard labor is a highly developed taste for local intercoastal hangout Captain Hiram's grouper sandwiches, a penchant for Crown Royal and a dwindling fund to support their diving habit. But, as they suit up to begin the first dive of the day there is salt in the air and salt in the sea and definitely salt in their veins. Mix in the sound of breaking surf, a summer sun and the prospect of finding sunken treasure and life is good.

Inside the surf-line with the water less than twelve feet deep and seas running six to eight feet Mallory dons his wet suit and scuba tank as he prepares to roll off the side of the boat. He points over his shoulder at the on/off air knob on the first stage of his regulator. "Johnson, see if my air is on; would you?"

Johnson checks, nods in the affirmative and gives Mallory a quick, unexpected nudge over the side. He can hear Mallory's muffled "Son-of-a-bitch" as he splashes into the deep. He laughs to himself; "Dumb ass! covers his Oceanic dive mask with one hand and follows his partner, fins first into the sea with a giant look-at-me-splash.

As soon as the two men are on the sandy bottom they set to work using a twelve-inch dredge nozzle attached to a ten-horsepower trash pump mounted on the boat above. Mallory vacuums the sea floor with the curved nozzle while Johnson continually monitors the attached nylon bag that filters the effluent for gold and silver.

Both men are over-weighted with lead to hold them fast to the bottom, but despite the extra lead they wear, every time a wave spills in the silt sand rolls heavily and whips them around in the zero visibility conditions.

"Son-of-a-bitch!" The muffled words explode from around Mallory's thick black rubber mouthpiece. Disturbed air bubbles roil skyward helter-skelter. A rogue wave has turned him unexpectedly topsy-turvy. He instinctively reaches out to steady himself on one of the craggy underwater boulders scattered across the ocean bed--boulders littered with spiny urchins —black-glass animals with sharp pointed spikes. Much like the medieval mace, the spines protrude in all directions.

Mallory had figured out a long time ago he didn't like these little nasty, prickly creatures of Neptune, but until today he'd tolerated them as a necessary nuisance, much like the reef sharks that occasionally bumped into him as he worked, to be avoided if possible, but not worth too much attention—an occupational hazard.

The thick steel-laced nylon gloves Mallory wears designed to protect his hands from the "black glass" perched on the rocks south of Sebastian Inlet have failed him. Bony black spines have penetrated his right glove and he again practices his new, favorite word several times in succession. "Son-of a-bitch, Son-of-a-bitch..."

Instinctively he jerks his arm up to his BC (buoyancy control device) to protect his injured hand and in the process drops his expensive hand-held magnetometer onto the ocean floor. He shakes his glove loose, inspects his damaged hand and is immediately roiled upside down once more by another wave crashing in. The abrupt subsequent tumble causes his head to whip back against the hard metal edge of the first stage of his regulator and disorients him. "Son-of-a-bitch!"

Before he can regain his composure and right himself he's thrown against a second boulder and in the process of catching himself grabs a handful of razor-sharp "black glass" in his now ungloved hand. The poisonous spines embed deep in his hand. This elicits another explosion of expletives which in turn loosens another round of excited, enriched air bubbles –a boiling cauldron destined for the surface.

As the poison from the Urchin hits his bloodstream Mallory is instantly sick to his stomach. The combination of being spun around upside down in the dark and the reaction to the allergen coursing through his body overwhelms him. He gives thumbs up in Johnson's general direction, forgets the "bends" and against every scuba rule he's ever learned, shoots straight for the surface.

Topside, Mallory drops his heavy lead weight belt, slips out of his inflated Oceanic BC and leaves it floating to fend for itself on the foamy sea, tugs his split fins off, slings them over the gunnels, and hoists himself up the ladder and over the stern of the boat and lands on his back with a thud. A loud grunt escapes his pursed lips. He unceremoniously yanks off his fogged-up mask, throws it in the general direction of the wheel and curses with a vengeance— "Son-of-a-bitch."

In case Johnson hasn't missed his sorry ass in the murky mess below, Mallory kills the dredge pump to alert his partner something's not right. Then he turns over to catch his breath. God almighty my hand hurts. Gas fumes leftover from the pump running fill his lungs and he realizes that this definitely is not a good idea. He lurches up, drapes himself over the gunnels and begins to chum the water in earnest. "Son-of-a-bitch!"

Johnson breaks the surface, pushes the inflator on his BC, pulls his mask down around his neck to keep it from washing away and surveys the situation with a practiced eye. He laughs raucously at Mallory's obvious discomfort and then taunts him. "I thought you were supposed to be worth a shit. I see you dropped your hand-held "mag". Did you drop your balls down there too?" Then he answers his own question. "Naw, I doubt you brought those along today—probably left 'em lying next to that skinny blonde slut you been hittin' every night since we got to the coast."

Mallory manages to stop chumming long enough to give Johnson the finger, peel off a husky heart-felt, "kiss-my-ass" and go right back to feeding the swirling pod of fish that have gathered for breakfast. He feels too bad to contend with his spite-filled buddy.

Johnson looks around, rolls his dark brown eyes at the sky and says to no one in particular, "I guess it's up to me to go back down there and find our expensive toy. Damn, this is some nasty-ass diving. I sure as hell hope it starts to pay off soon, 'cause I've enjoyed about all the fun I can stand." He spits in his mask to clear it, slides it back on, shoves the second stage of his Sherwood Magnum regulator back in his mouth, dumps the air from his BC and disappears beneath the waves in a storm of bubbles.

Mallory glances in his general direction and mutters a stifled, "Good riddance, you miserable son-of-a-bitch. I hope a shark bites your damned lips off."

When Johnson surfaces the second time he triumphantly holds the recovered hand-held mag over his head in a tight-fisted grip. He clambers over the side of the boat, slides out of his gear, unhooks the effluent bag full of sand and shell coupled to his BC and offhandedly tosses it toward a deserted corner of the deck.

His humor much improved he looks his partner's injured hand over and says, "Let me see that hand, Mallory."

Mallory resists.

Johnson unstraps a small dive-knife from his chest sleeve, and this time with authority barks, "Damn it, Mallory, give me your hand. You know as well as I do that glass has got to come out."

Mallory pays him no attention. He's already decided, dying is the only option that makes sense. In fact, the thought he'll die soon is all that's keeps him alive. In exasperation Johnson grabs Mallory by the arm and growls, "Gimme that injured paw." He twists Mallory's hand sideways, hard—hard and rough, and sets it across his knee. Mallory is too feverish and dizzy to fight back.

Johnson probes the razor-sharp knife blade into the soft palm his partner's hand.

Mallory winces. "Son-of-a-bitch."

The blade makes an audible bone-chilling rasp as it grates against a glass spine. Eventually when enough blood and curses are spilled, Johnson has managed to dig out all the black shards and throw them overboard. He looks up at Mallory and grins an evil grin and taunts, "Better you than me partner."

As the poison in his system recedes, Mallory begins to feel better. His breathing returns to normal, his pulse steadies and his dark green eyes begin to glitter with intent. Without warning, he throws a quick knotted left jab that bloodies Johnson's nose and jibes back, "That's to even the score for your smart-ass comment about my woman, Dani."

Johnson reels back smacking his head against the port gunnel. He gingerly cups his bloodied nose in his calloused hands, and spits out a bloody froth on the deck and shouts," Shit, Mallory, what in hell is wrong with you? Have you lost your mind?"

Mallory stares past Johnson ignoring his partner's deep distress and stammers, "Do you see that Johnson?" He nods in the direction of the salt-caked net bag thrown carelessly aside. He shakes Johnson by the shoulder. "Do you see? Do you see?"

Johnson is way past being in the mood for one of Mallory's puerile games. "See what? Have you lost your ever-loving mind?" He stops mid-breath and in spite of his trepidation at being the butt of another of Mallory's jokes can't help himself and turns in the direction his partner is indicating. Gold sparkles in the effluent mesh bag. "Well, I'll be a son-of-a-bitch! "

In a furious rush the divers reach for their treasure simultaneously, bang their heads together and fall back, laughing uncontrollably, beating their feet and fist against the flat bottom of the boat.

Mallory winks at Johnson, whistles happily and quips. "Son-of-a-bitch; now, ain't that a pretty sight?"

Mallory and Kieran

Mallory felt the tremor. He'd felt tremors before, but this one was different than anything he'd ever experienced. He was a treasure diver and long ago had learned to expect and accept the strange and unusual ways of the sea. However, this time he'd been caught off guard and as the tremor struck home again and again and rattled his table his quiet thoughts scattered out into the balmy Caribbean night air. Curious, he looked up to see the source.

A slight, dirty-blonde in a long, white cotton dress bore down on him with a set of fierce blue eyes, lit up by torch light and wine—eyes the color of the waves crashing in against the rocky Brac beach.

Her mouth was open and working and working quite well, but Mallory couldn't hear a thing, but he had no trouble reading her lips perfectly. "You rude, arrogant, bastard, what's the matter with you? My friend, Shelley, and I have invited you to join us at our table three times. All you do is stare out lost into the dark. You looked so melancholy we thought you might like company. Obviously, we were wrong, but you could've at least acknowledged our offer and said no thank you."

Mallory responded with a big white toothy grin and held his hands out palms up, "I apologize, I have a busted left ear drum and can't hear a word on the side facing you and your friend. In fact, I can barely hear at all. Forgive me and…please…don't hit my table again. I ain't scared of nothing, but you just scared the hell out of me."

The blonde held her hand out and said, "Sorry, I had no idea. My name is Kieran and my friend there is Shelley. We're on vacation from Juneau looking for salty breezes and warm men and adventure in the sun and not necessarily in that order."

Mallory laughed at Kieran's straightforward manner, which caused his ear to throb. Despite the pain and not hearing well he couldn't resist engaging Kieran in a little friendly banter. He liked the sparkle in her eyes. "Too bad you're not looking for a salty man, warm sun and adventure in the wind; I could be of some help to you with that request.

The girls were definitely in full party mode and Mallory—well, Mallory was always ready. He slid his plastic chair over, introduced himself formally to Shelley and the three of them soon had a dozen empty glasses sitting in front of them on the round table.

Mallory leaned in to draw the women closer. "So, tell me the truth, what do you ladies do when you're not harassing innocent victims on faraway islands in paradise?"

Shelley was shy and to make up for her friends' quiet manner, Kieran was doubly ebullient. "Guess: What do I look like?"

Mallory was afraid to answer that question directly, so he went for off-the-wall. "I'm pretty sure you're a camel jockey. I mean, you're strong and your hair matches the desert sand and from the way you came at me earlier I'll bet one of your dromedary friends taught you to spit."

He stopped to see how his remarks were being digested and continued when Kieran didn't take a swing. "Or maybe you're a mermaid and live in the sea in a deep cave—that would explain the deep clearness of your cerulean eyes; and you've only come ashore for one night to seduce a poor sailor and drag him unawares into your lair as a trophy to impress Poseidon."

Mallory paused and studied the expression on Kieran's face and for a moment he believed he had uncovered her secret.

Kieran stared furiously back through intense blue-diamond eyes, raised one eyebrow and completely captivated Mallory's heart with her next seductive remark. "I've come for you Mallory. Are you ready? The sea is calling you; listen, can you hear her? She wants you, she needs you, she's waiting for you to mount her and ride her fine form and dive deep into her depths and drown in her mysteries and let her crests enfold you and strangle you until you are hers, all hers and nobody else's—hers and hers alone."

A stunned Mallory stuttered, "Who…who in the hell are you?"

Kieran slapped the table and giggled. "I had you going didn't I Mallory, I could see it in your eyes when I was talking, I am right, the sea is your lover and true love and you wish all I said was true and could be true and will be true; it's your dream."

Again, Mallory was stunned. How could this stranger know all this about him already? Who was she, really? "I don't understand, how can you be so sure? We've just met."

Shelley yawned and said, "If the two of you will excuse me I've got a bed to catch and dream to chase. Besides the two of you have a long night ahead and you won't need me for the final burst. Good night, Mallory, nice to make your acquaintance." She rolled her eyes at Kieran as she stood up. "And don't be too hard on this poor man; I think he might actually like your acerbic tongue." She winked at Mallory and ambled off under the gibbous moon and coconut palms toward a thatched tourist hut.

Kieran was the first to break the silence that drifted in. "Well, now that that's settled why don't we stroll on down to one of those double hammocks they've got strung out along the beach and take in the night and get to know each other in a more enlightened way."

Mallory was intrigued and excited by the notion. He pushed his squeaky chair back, stood up, shrugged his shoulders, whistled under his breath and followed Kieran—what else could he do, he'd never heard of a man saying no to a mermaid; especially not to a mermaid with a woman's legs and especially not to a mermaid with a pair of legs like Kieran's.

As they ambled toward the beach, the rhythmic sway of Kieran's heart-shaped ass hypnotized Mallory. He wondered if they'd talk first or if they'd talk after or if they'd talk at all. Mallory had never done it with a mermaid in a hammock.

Riding shotgun with Sam
A Memoir

I got a phone call from my daughter, Joy—not unexpected. "Dad, I know you're headed to St. Augustine this weekend to see Shane, will you do me a favor?"

"Sure, baby girl. Whadda you need?"

"Your granddaughter, Sara, is begging to go with you to visit Rebecca."

"No problem, honey, she's welcome to ride up with me. You know how much I love her. Is that all?"

"No, actually, Dad, that's not the favor." I can hear the long hesitation while she gathers her courage. "Would you be willing to take Papa Sam along too? You know he can't get around by himself anymore. He's been here for the last month sitting around in the same spot doing nothing, largely ignored, and I think it's time he got out. Frankly, I'm afraid something will happen to him if he stays here much longer and I'll be the one to catch the blame."

"Have you talked to your brother about this? I mean is he willing to have your Papa Sam come and stay for a few days?"

"Yeah, I've discussed it with my brother and Mom; they both agree with me. Shane is planning to drive to Tennessee for the reunion next month and since the rest of us are flying we thought it would be better if Papa Sam rode with Shane from St. Augustine to Chattanooga. He never did like flying. If you'll take him part of the way to Shane's, it'll save me a special trip."

"Okay, I'll probably leave out about ten o'clock Saturday morning for Rebecca's birthday party, will you please have your Papa Sam and Sara ready to go. I hate getting a late start."

"No problem, they'll be ready."

That's how Sam came to ride shotgun with me on a cloudless autumn day in 2013. Seven-year-old Sara was excited, as usual to be headed to see her first cousin, Rebecca, who is a year younger and three inches taller and looks up to her vivacious older brown-eyed dynamo cousin with adoration bordering awe.

Sara is waiting for me in the driveway when I arrive and immediately begins to issue orders, "Papa Rod, I wanna listen to 'Three Little Monkeys, Momma says Jacob can't go; he's going to see Thomas the Train with Grammy. Can I have a chocolate kiss? Are we there yet?"

All this and I haven't even knocked on the door. It's going to be a long ride to St. Augustine. Joy walks into her garage and greets me, "Thank you so much Daddy. It's such a big relief to know Papa Sam is in good hands, even if he won't say so, I know he appreciates the ride."

"Happy to help, baby girl, where is he?"

"Come on in, Daddy, Papa Sam's in the dining room. Can I get you something to drink, a glass of sweet tea?"

"No, honey, why don't you walk your grandfather out and get him situated in the passenger seat of the truck while I give Jake a big hug. I want to see my grandson before I hit the road."

Four-year-old Jake comes rumbling around the corner, flashing his big bright blue eyes holding James and Diesel and begins to jabber away about his upcoming adventure to ride a real train in Cordele, Georgia. "Hey Papa, I'm going with Grammy to ride Thomas the Train, do you wanna see my new train tracks?"

"Absolutely, Jake, show Papa what you've made." After a stellar review of Jake's new engineering marvel, it's time to hit the road. "Come on Sara, quit doddling."

She gets settled into the backseat with Rebecca's present and barks new orders before I can crank the truck. "Go get my blanky Papa, I forgot it."

Her mother, Joy, who has just finished strapping Papa Sam in, snips, "Stop it, Sara. Don't talk to Papa Rod that way or you're not going anywhere. I'll get your blanket for you."

Papa Sam sits quietly through the whole exchange without a single quack, one of his favorite things to do when somebody does or says something silly—quack like a duck. He's in another world at the moment and ignoring our petty shenanigans. I'm pretty sure he's happy just to be outside in the fresh air, headed toward Tennessee. He has no interest in the inane.

Joy returns with Sara's blanket. "Thanks again, Daddy," She reaches in and gives her grandfather a pat, looks lovingly down at him and pleads with me, "Please take good care of Papa Sam, you know how fragile he is these days. And, Sara, I'd better not hear about any mischief, young lady."

I back out and instinctively reach over to steady Sam, as though he's a mere child and head down the bumpy, dirt road my daughter lives on. It seems a little strange to see Sam without a cup of black coffee and a Pall Mall stuck between his lips; he gave 'em both up a while back, but I remember how fond he was of telling me, and anybody else that would stop for two seconds and listen to his Samisms, how he liked his coffee like his women, black, strong and extra sweet.

~

Sam met his future wife, Joy, who is not black, but is strong and extra sweet, in Tennessee and ran off with her to Ringgold, Georgia in the middle of the night, in nineteen-fifty-two, in a '48 Ford and got married. It was illegal to wed in Tennessee at sixteen, but Georgia was a lot more relaxed than Tennessee about what age breeding should be considered legal. Joy's brothers agreed with the state of Tennessee, so Sam and his new bride kept heading south on 441 to Florida to avoid dying and to also save his newly acquired brothers-in-law from the electric chair in Georgia.

Sam confided to me one afternoon after three vodka and orange juices, "You have to believe me when I say, if you'd seen my wife when she was sixteen you'd have grabbed her too. She was so hot, she raised the temperature in Orlando another ten degrees when we moved here—global warming my ass."

Besides his wife and children, Victoria, and Vince, and his grandchildren, Sam loved three things: all-night poker games, all-night three cushion billiard games, and a little curly-haired black fellow named Jock—actually I think he loved Jock more than the rest. He was pure-bred and loved Sam as much as Sam loved him. When Jock went blind at fourteen and subsequently died, Sam grieved for years. He was sure it was his fault—if only he'd gotten him to the Vet sooner he was sure he could have been saved.

~

"Papa Rod, turn up the radio, I can't hear my songs."

Instead of his usual quick quack to tell his great granddaughter to sit still, Sam has nothing to say. I look over at him and shake my head;

just when you think nothing will ever change, everything does. "Okay, Sara, hold your horses. We're about to get on the interstate do you want something to eat? Do you need to go potty?" I'm greeted by sullen silence. "If you're hungry you better say so now or you ain't gonna get a bite of nothing for the next two hours."

"Steak'n'Shake, Steak'n'Shake, I want Steak'n'Shake, Pleeaase, Papa!"

Sam is oblivious to the conversation, so I think what the heck if he don't care I don't care. "Okay, Miss Sara, have it your way." I'm just not used to Sam being so quiet. It's eerie.

Once through the drive thru and up on the interstate I turn to Sam, "Well, we're finally headed North, that oughta make you happy." A semi tractor-trailer passes too close and brings my eyes back to the road; I'm not sure, but Sam may have finally cracked a smile.

~

Not long after he and Joy moved to Orlando, Sam went to work for Morrisons Downtown Cafeteria and fell into the habit of stopping off at the local pool hall around the corner after work. He had talent and before too long he'd become adept at three cushion billiards and began to spend more time at Joe Gill's, gambling, than he did at home. His new bride was soon leading the life of a pool widow.

One night, after repeatedly promising his wife he'd be home early for supper Sam stopped off at a local gambling parlor, Sportstown, and got into a game of Gin. Time slipped away and it was after midnight when Sam came home broke. But, true to form his dutiful and forgiving bride had waited up for him and kept his meal warmed so they could eat together. Sam sat down at the table, stuck a fork in his food and said, "Joy, these potatoes are cold, can you do something about it?"

Without missing a beat, Joy walked over to the table, picked the plate up, whirled around and threw his late supper across the kitchen. It landed against the opposite wall and exploded on the flowered wallpaper halfway between a black rimmed clock, appropriated from a local Morrisons under renovation, and the open trash can below. The plate was followed into the garbage can by an amalgam of ketchup, milk gravy, broccoli, potatoes, and country fried chicken that oozed slowly down the wall, drop by drop, in sync with the silent tick tock of the clock.

Sam's response, "Damn, Joy," did not impress his wife. The paisley print couch had proved less than comfortable for the next few nights.

~

"**S**am, do you remember the night you wiped everybody out at the poker table and then gave us all our money back so you could keep the game going and then wiped us all out again." I've never seen Sam so quiet, not even when he was sulking.

Sara pipes up. "Are we there yet?"

"Another 30 minutes. We're passing Palm Coast now."

"Can you please hurry, Papa, I'm bored. I wanna play with Rebecca."

"We'll be there soon. Sit back and relax."

"Are we there yet?"

~

When Fidel Castro threatened to blow Florida off the map with nuclear weapons in 1962, Sam had a bomb shelter installed in his backyard at 224 South Lawsona Boulevard in Orlando. Shortly afterwards he stocked it full of food and liquor and mischief and playing cards. A fresh-air filtration system was a major feature of the hideout—which made it the perfect late-night spot for heavy drinkers and smokers who liked to gamble.

Characters like Fast Eddie, who won a bet from a private dick named Chuck regarding the length of a particular part of his anatomy, were regulars at the game—Fast Eddie laid the subject of the bet on the table and proved that ten inches ain't as nearly as impossible as you might think.

And of course, the game wouldn't have been complete without the Orlando Chief of Police, who was forced to leave his gun on a hook in the house so he wouldn't be tempted to arrest other players whose pictures appeared from time to time on post office walls—this was Sam's circle. On a good night the chimney could have competed with any winter fireplace in the country.

A few years later, I had the privilege of playing cards with Sam a couple of times a week at my office on a red-topped table given to me by Morris Letsinger of Letsinger Produce and restored by Sam.

Back then, Sam was quite a talker. "Man, can you believe what that crazy nut, Max did?" Sam looked around the table at me the other three players to see if he could get anyone else to agree with his statement. Sam had just bluffed with an ace high against Max's two-pair showing and got him to fold. Max had jumped up and stalked away and Sam was looking to see if anyone else was as amused as he was—they weren't. We'd all been taken to the cleaners at one point or another by him.

"Come on, Max, I was just lucky. Come on back, man. Don't act like that I'll give you another chance to get even."

Max's expected retort was the extended middle finger of his right hand in Sam's direction. "Kiss my ass, you redneck hillbilly."

This brought laughter and hoots and relieved the tension. Sam answer was to finish cleaning Max out the next hand.

Max didn't take losing lightly and one night while we were playing cards he got even with Sam. He arranged to have the Parliament House, a local gay hangout, call the office and ask for Sam by name. They said he'd left his wallet there the night before. Max made sure everyone could hear the conversation on the speaker phone; this time a flustered Sam had no problem getting everyone at the game to laugh.

~

Sam remains clammed up. I suppose he knows this is his last trip through Florida. He can't drive anymore and I'm sure he recognizes the fact that after he's moved to his boyhood home: the state of Tennessee, he won't pass this way again. I know he's anxious to be home with the rest of his kin, but at the moment I think he's contented to watch the Florida landscape roll away beneath him one final time. I decide to leave him be and concentrate on the road.

As we reach our exit on I-95, on the north side of St. Augustine, Sara begins to jump up and down in the back seat; she knows we're getting close to our destination. "Are we there yet?"

"Almost."

"Are we there yet?"

"I said almost. What's the matter with you? Sit down and be quiet."

"Are we there yet?"

It feels strange to think I probably won't see Sam again after today. I don't get to Tennessee often. It suddenly strikes me, I'm about to part, forever, with a valued part of my life—someone who's been a part of my life, most of my life—someone even my parents knew when he was a boy.

~

My folks came to know him because his older sister, Katherine, was married to Howard Russell, the pastor of the Zellwood Church of God where we attended services. My dad laughed whenever he told the story about little Sam riding his bicycle up and down King Street in front of the church during services and making faces at the congregation as they came out. He was a rebel even back then.

Over the years not much had changed about Sam as far as attending church went, but one exceptional thing did happen as he got older, he became quite the woodworking craftsman and began to build beautiful, detailed replicas of all the churches his Uncle had pastored. Perhaps you can learn a good deal from the outside looking in.

~

After he was married and living back in Florida, Sam's daughter, Victoria, came to share my bed when she was only six months old—I was four. One lazy Sunday afternoon, after church, when Pastor Russell and Katherine came to visit, they brought her brother Sam and his young wife, Joy, and their baby girl, Victoria, along to meet my parents. Baby Victoria took a nap in my bed just before the excitement got underway—another seventeen years would pass before she shared my bed again.

Not long after Victoria was put down for her nap my older brother, Richard's wife, Millicent, came running into the house in a panic with her two-year-old her daughter Sheila in her arms. "She's going to die. Oh, my God, oh my God, she's going to die. She's swallowed kerosene. Oh, my God!" She shoved Sheila at my older brother who stared back at his hysterical wife in shocked silence and disbelief; he had no clue what to do.

The whole house went into a tizzy. My sister-in-law stood there crying and yelling and wringing her hands, while Pastor Russell jumped up and gawked and Daddy started for the phone to call Doctor Williams and my poor glassy-eyed brother gazed down helplessly at his daughter.

My mother, Miriam, calmly stepped in, "Here, give her to me." She took my niece in her arms, turned her upside down and got her to empty the contents of her stomach and then gave her a dose of I-still-ain't-sure-what and went right back to her conversation with Sister Katherine Russell about the sad state of affairs on the way certain women had started to dress for church.

The incident was so traumatic that years later when Victoria and I started to date, her Mother, Joy, recalled the grandmother, my momma, and the nap her daughter had taken that day in my bed. It's a shame that not long after Victoria and I got married that sweet lady Katherine was taken ill with a brain tumor and died young.

~

Sara already has her seatbelt off and is jumping up and down in the backseat as we turn on to Cousin Rebecca's street, Wild Palm Court. Her chant begins anew, "Are we there yet? Are we there yet? Are we there yet?"

"Well, Sam, I'm happy we could travel this far together, it's been quite a trip, but I ain't able to go no further with you." He has no comment. His grandson, Shane greets us in the driveway of his two-story home. I open my door and release Sara into the wild as my six-foot-four-inch son walks up to me and throws his arms around me and gives me a big hug and a kiss. He looks through the driver's side window across the seat at his Papa Sam and says, "Thank you so much, Dad, for bringing Papa Sam this far. I really appreciate it."

"You're welcome, Son. How about you go around and help your grandfather out of the car. He didn't seem to mind the trip, but it has been a long ride."

"Sure, Dad, I'd be glad to. Did Papa Sam quack at you on the way up? If you're thirsty, I think Stef has a pot of coffee on."

"Sounds good, I could use a cup, too bad your Papa had to give up coffee and no, if you can believe it, he didn't quack once the whole morning."

He throws an answer back over the cab of my Tundra as he opens the passenger door. "Yeah, that is hard to believe." He reaches in and unfastens his Papa Sam's restraint and tenderly says, "Come on; let's get you inside, Papa." He lifts him gently from the seat. "It won't be long now; you'll be home soon."

Shane starts up the sidewalk toward his front door holding Papa Sam close, so he doesn't slip and fall and then, pauses and looks over at me with a faraway smile on his face as though he's suddenly found buried treasure. He tenderly strokes the cold ceramic urn at rest in his hands and says wistfully, "You did have quite a journey, didn't you Papa Sam?"

Dedicated to the memory of:

Sam C. Haston

In the Time of Two Moons

"Please, tell me the story again, Grandma."

"Which story, Sweetie? It's late—time for sleep and dreams."

She pulls the comforter up close under Lil's chin. "Tomorrow is a school day and you need to rest. Close your eyes—we'll have that story another time."

"Please, Grandma I haven't heard the story about the time of two moons since I was a little girl. Please, Grandma, please."

Grandma Ali strokes Lil's dark, curly hair. "It's terribly late young lady, but if you promise to study the back of your eyelids, breathe deep and use all the imagination you possess," She hesitates. "I'll do my best to recall how the heavens looked when I was seventeen."

"I remember the night the second moon appeared—it was a night much like this one. I lived in Oregon with my mother, my father, three cats, a parakeet and the orneriest hound dog that ever was. The house we lived in had a second story window that faced west and overlooked the sea—that was my room." She continues to stroke Lil's hair with her extraordinary hands.

"I was sitting in my window seat dreaming of a boy while I watched the surf roll in and crash against the rocks—a full moon

69

reflected the scene. Dolphins rode the crest of the waves along the shore and in the distance a large mother whale guarded her calf as she sent water spouts soaring fifty feet into the cold air; it was a glorious night—a magical night—a night I shall never forget."

Grandma Ali pauses, but Lil is anxious. "Go on, Grandma, please don't stop."

"Patience, child," She pulls Lil's covers up snug. "It was a long time ago. Give me a minute to remember. You want the whole story, don't you?"

"Oh yes, Grandma."

"Good girl." Grandma Ali resumes her story in a voice, faraway and haunted. Her eyes and heart begin to drift back. She sees another time and hears another voice—a voice strange to earthborn ears—a voice that exists deep in her soul—a comforting whisper—a longing angst.

"It appeared from nowhere—a second moon on the horizon—smooth, translucent, without craters. The western sky filled with a new light—a light of renewed hope. Don't ask me how I knew, I knew. Seated on my window cushion, I was bathed in that living light and I knew."

"Certain peace infused me as I continued to gaze on the beauty before me and I could feel my mind open. And then…there was chaos. Sirens rang out all over town. Police cruisers and fire trucks clogged the streets. Mother rushed in and hurried me downstairs to huddle with the rest of the family in the den. They were all afraid.

The television blared—fear etched on the news anchor's face. My dog howled and paced. Panic permeated the conversation in our close room—our world had been rudely awakened from lethargic slumber."

That sounds so scary, Grandma. Weren't you afraid?"

Ali gently touches her granddaughter's face. "No, dear heart, strangely enough I wasn't. Most people are frightened of change, but I embraced it; not because I was braver, but because all my young life I'd been waiting—expecting something momentous to occur—to be a part of a great transformation I knew must surely come."

Lil looks admiringly at her grandmother. "I hope when I am older, I'm as brave as you Grandma."

"When the time comes you will be, Lil, you will be." She smiles at her granddaughter. "And braver, I promise. Then I heard my name being called from faraway. It wasn't loud like you might expect, but rather quiet and gentle and insistent. It was beautiful and resonant—a male voice that encouraged me to come outside—to come to him—to be with him."

"I wasn't sure how to proceed, but I couldn't resist. The pull was strong. I slipped out of the house. No one noticed. The rest of the family was too fixated on the rumor-driven screen in front of them. As I started to walk down the sidewalk in the direction of the voice I noticed that I had begun to feel different—lighter, so light in fact that when I looked down I realized I was now weightless, high above the ground, wrapped in a beam of light emanating from the new moon."

"That is so cool, Grandma. Could anyone else see you?"

"No, that was the most interesting thing, to me, Lil; no one could see me because I was bathed in light and had become a part of the light. I'm not sure I can explain it to you better, but I know that's how it was. Soon, instead of walking, I was gliding effortlessly toward the welcome of the moon glow."

~

For the better part of an hour Commander So-Ir had watched ALI, from the top observatory level of his ship. He could have transported her much faster through the light, but he wanted extra time to examine her.

She was the loveliest creature he had ever seen—and he had traveled through over fifty different galaxies. She was perfect in physical proportion, but most importantly, through his oculus, he could see deep into her mind and it too was perfect.

The ALI had been chosen carefully. Years of interstellar and black hole flights from his home planet Zargon had been expended searching for the Worthy One. Finally, located the year before, the Worthy One—the ALI was about to enter his ship. He felt honored to have been charged with such a mission.

He turned to his second in command, Captain DIL. "Bring the ALI to me as soon as she is on board—and tell Science Chief REMI he is free to commence Operation Cleanse—the sooner the better—this archaic, acidic planet is in dire need of clean up."

"Yes, Commander."

Finally, So-Ir thinks, the Alien Life Instrument is about to arrive. He turns his head slightly and speaks into his shoulder-mounted communicator—his voice audible to everyone on board. "To all crew members, greetings, this is an historic day for all who cherish our way of life, an opportunity to offer another planet a way forward into the future. But, as with all beginnings, there must be endings." Here he pauses and breathes deeply. "Do your duty. Science Chief REMI will be in charge. Follow his orders explicitly—they come directly from the Quadrivium."

~

"What happened next, Grandma?"

Commander So-Ir, who spoke perfect English, was the first to introduce himself to me. He was there to greet me as the beam of light ushered me into the moon.

"What was he like, Grandma—the Commander?"

Patience child, I'm coming to that. He was tall and well-built with thick, wavy black hair and large almond-shaped eyes set wide apart—handsome by Earth standards. He extended a refined hand, apparently a universal gesture of goodwill—it seemed natural, so I took it.

Immediately, I noticed he had six slender fingers—not misshapen as I would have expected, but instead in direct proportion to his hand—more natural in appearance than five fingers are to my own hand."

Lil giggles. "I like him already."

Shush, this is a bedtime story. I'll do the talking, young lady. If you wish me to continue, be still."

"Sorry, Grandma."

"I wanted to ask a thousand questions, but before I could ask a single one, Commander So-Ir interrupted me."

"I'll answer all your questions in due time, ALI."

"What a relief, I thought. He didn't even get your name right. How foolish to think he might be reading your mind."

"I'm sorry, Shauna," he spoke gently, "if you prefer I will call you by your current Earth name. In time I hope you will come to accept your new designation: ALI."

I was taken aback. "H-How d-do you kn-know my n-name?"

"I know everything about you. Actually, I know, or I should say my personal mechanical servant or MS knows everything about every living organism on your filthy planet. Don't let that concern you. I assure you, you are safe. My sector of the galaxy has been studying your world for centuries and until recently saw no reason to interfere. Now, it seems we have little choice."

"Interfere, what do you intend to do?"

"I don't mean to be insensitive, but your planet is filthy and in order for it to survive it must be cleaned and rebooted—a fresh beginning—a new Eden."

"A new Eden, who are you, God?"

"Hardly. However, I've already given my Science Chief, REMI, orders to start Operation Cleanse and there is no power on your planet that can stop what must be done. We intend to scrub every atom of your planet from the deepest ocean upward into the atmosphere—nothing will be left as it is."

"Is there nothing that can be done to save us? What about my parents and my house and my dog, what will happen to them?"

"That is precisely why you are here, ALI—to save your planet from the corruption and destruction that the entities you call corporations have rained down on Earth for years in the name of monetary profits. There is no need to concern yourself, provisions have been made—your loved ones are safe."

"I'm only seventeen, what can I possibly do?"

"Everything—the success of my mission—the survival of planet Earth—depend ultimately on you. Come, take my hand, I want to show you a place—a special place of emotional truth and purity that will allow you to understand your role in the future of Earth."

~

"I'm starting to get a little sleepy, Grandma. How much longer is your story? I don't want to miss anything."

"Not much more now, Lil. I've been saving the best for last. Commander So-Ir took my hand and led me through his giant moon ship over a great distance. How we traveled so far so fast with no visible

74

means of transport, I still have no idea. He tried to explain the technology, but I was so enthralled with his beautiful voice and my ethereal surroundings that I did not understand as I should have—I was captivated."

"At his request, I followed him through a door labeled SPORE, which I later learned meant Seed Pods Ordered to Rejuvenate Earth. I remember being overcome with a distinct sense of the future in that moment. Then he led me through a veil of pink light into another room where the air tasted of sweet perfume—romantic music swelled the walls."

"Commander So-Ir gently guided me to a couch of pure light, put his arm around me and confided his hope that Earth should be reborn and what part he desired that I should play. I was destined to become part of an adventure that would change the Earth forever. Only later did I realize my heart and mind were being controlled—no, directed is the better word. Nothing ever happened against my wishes."

"What does that mean, Grandma?"

Grandma Ali is quiet for a moment before she continues, "It means I fell in love with a man from another world—a world and a man that exist only in my dreams." She kisses Lil on the forehead. "Now, if your curiosity is satisfied, sleep tight."

"How did you get home, Grandma?"

"The light, child—the light brought me home."

~

"Commander So-Ir, sorry to interrupt, but it's time."

"Thank you, Captain DIL." He slips out of the bed of light he has shared with the ALI for over a month and gently kisses her sleeping lips. "See to it that she arrives home safely, Captain. I'm no good at goodbye. It will be better if she awakes in her own bed."

"Yes sir, it shall be so. Oh, and, Sir, does she know?"

"She is the Worthy One—the ALI, of course she knows. Ask Science Chief REMI to report to me on the observatory deck. And plot a course for Zargon. I'm longing forward to ebony flowers and purple skies."

"Yes, Sir."

Science Chief REMI enters the observatory deck. "You sent for me, Commander."

"Yes. Your mission was successful?"

"Yes, of course."

I am: Replenish Earth Mission One. The Quadrivium programmed me for the sole purpose of cleansing Earth—failure would have been impossible. The mission is complete—Earth has been meticulously scrubbed."

"I apologize, Science Chief, I sometimes forget that I'm the only Organic on board this vessel."

Science Chief REMI continues, "Sir, Earth's ability to produce their inferior GMO's has been permanently destroyed, oil spills are spotless, ozone levels are normal, the land and oceans are again pristine, honey bees are thriving and fresh water wells across the planet spring forth untainted—planet Earth has been restored to optimal condition. But, Commander, there is one thing I do not understand—the carbon-based units that created the damage have been left untouched."

"That's true, Science Chief. The Quadrivium cannot assume the role of Ultimate Creator. They can only hope the stern warnings we have delivered to those in power across Earth combined with our obvious capability to destroy them, should we wish, may modify their behavior for some time to come. We sow superior seeds and hope for a fruitful harvest." He is suddenly tired. "That will be all Science Chief."

"So it is, Commander."

As Commander So-Ir takes one last look at the planet he has come to restore a rare feeling overtakes him—he wishes the Ali was standing beside him. He hadn't meant to fall in love—it wasn't like him. A professional hazard, he supposes. One last look—the doors on the observatory close. He touches his communicator and speaks one word to Captain DIL, Deliverer of Intergalactic Light, "Go."

~

Ali rises from her sleeping granddaughter's bedside. At eighty she doesn't spring so fast anymore. Lil's bedroom window is cracked open and as she moves to close out the draft she looks away into the star-bright heavens and prays the same prayer she has prayed since she was a girl of seventeen: "Keep him safe and if it be your will bring him to me again." Moonlight reflected on the horizon causes her heart to skip a beat.

She sighs and moves back into the room to turn off the bedside lamp and thinks how much Lil reminds her of herself at that age—and him. He had expressed strenuously to her during their time together that the future of Earth would depend on a life—a light infused life—Ali knows he was right.

One of Lil's slender hands has wandered out from under the covers—with loving tenderness Ali strokes her granddaughter's hand and places her six, slender fingers back under the warmth of her comforter one by one. "Sleep well, my love—my Lil—sleep well."

Fit 'ems
A Christmas Tale

The Holiday Season is upon us and the weight of what and why we celebrate soon settles in on each of us. Most of us will be wrapped in the glittering rush—Christmas truths obfuscated in a whirlwind of shopping and parties.

Store windows will reflect and record our lines of stress as we spend our hard-earned dollars at corporate cash registers. But, it's after Christmas that the real excitement begins; a headlong flight to exchange garments, handbags, etc., et al—wrong color, wrong fashion, too small, too big, too...

The giver of the gift and the love behind the gift lost in the post-holiday hustle and bustle. It's easy to hurt a friend or family member when we return the thing they've given us rather than honor the gift by receiving it in the spirit of love it was given.

During this time of year my memory invariably returns to a Christmas story my ninety-year-old father once shared with me—the story of a gift given to a wise and humble man more than 75 years ago—a man who honored the gift he received with grace and dignity.

During the Great Depression Daddy worked six days a week from can 'til can't—sunup to sundown—for a dollar a day in the Florida orange groves and packing houses. It was hard labor, full of sore muscles, little pay, and less thanks.

One of the men he worked alongside, an enterprising young man from Kentucky named Johnny, had worn so many holes in his only pair of boots that he had to resort to layering the inside of his soles with cardboard to keep the sugar sand and thorns from tearing at his feet. He couldn't afford a new pair of shoes—he had too many mouths to feed on his meager salary.

As it so happened, the wealthy grove owner, they worked for, also owned an interest in a successful, thriving shoe factory up North. He wasn't a callous man and he had taken notice of the poor condition of Johnny's foot wear. He decided that, as a Christmas present, he would present Johnny with a pair of boots.

Instead of new boots, however, he decided that because of the economic hardship of the times, the prudent thing to do would be to pass on a pair of his own well-worn work shoes that he'd grown tired of wearing.

Daddy related. "You'd have thought a man who owned a shoe factory would've at least give Johnny a new pair of shoes." Then he laughed. "But, that man was so tight he squeaked when he walked."

As my father continued to tell his story I agreed, why in the world would the Grove Owner, who owned a shoe factory risk insult a valued hand with a used pair of boots when he could have so easily afforded to give him new ones.

The real rub, though, was that Johnny had a size 8 foot and the boots he was presented with were size 12's. He had already endured more than his fair share of ribbing from the men he worked with because of his small feet and now the too-large-to-wear gift added more unwanted fuel to an already hot fire.

Under the circumstances, Johnny could have easily taken insult or, at the very least, resented the used, too-large-to-wear boots. But, Johnny had a completely different view of the gift he had been presented.

The day after Christmas Johnny showed up at work and to everyone's surprise he was wearing his new boots. He had figured out that if he wadded up enough old newspaper and stuffed it into the toe the extra space would be filled, and he could comfortably wear his Christmas gift.

When others invariably poked fun at the boots, Johnny would lift his feet, one at the time, to show off his new footwear and opine in his long, drawn-out, Southern drawl, "You fellas can see for yourself, these brogans may be scuffed up some, but they've got plenty of sole left. Yes, sir, I am right proud of 'em." Then he'd shake a raised foot in all directions. "Look how snug they fit. Yes sir, these boots is the perfect size. These boots is 'fit 'ems'."

Hoover Days, as Daddy referred to the Great Depression, didn't last forever and by the time I came along in the 1950's Johnny was a self-made millionaire, yet he remained a man of great humility, thankful for gifts, great and small, the rest of his life—an example to us all.

The Christmas season offers an excellent opportunity to seek peace and reconciliation. Perhaps this year, like Daddy's old Kentucky friend, Johnny, we will pause for a moment in the crush of the crowds and find a place of inner stillness, a place of humility—a place where we will give thanks for the grace that the Christ child born in a manger has bestowed upon each of us— the gifts of peace and love—our own personal *"fit'ems"*.

The Hunted

Raven swims long, languorous, refined strokes up and down the nearly deserted Lakeside Inn pool. It's early April and she has come to Florida to escape the withering winter snows of the mountainous Northeast and the withering looks of an insipid man, which is to say, a romance that had withered before it had hardly begun.

She swims with the practiced ease of a trained athlete turning her head from side to side as she breathes in rhythm with her crawl and each time, as she approaches her flip turn, her head rises and turns west—her beautiful, wide-open, emerald-green eyes locked on Raeburn's crystal-blue, intrigued gaze.

~

Six-year-old Raeburn takes a running leap and fearlessly bails off into the deep end of the city swimming pool where he promptly sinks like a rock. As his feet settle onto the rough concrete bottom, he involuntarily gives a huge, panicked push and shoots toward the surface. As he rises he looks up and sees the bright sky and wonders to himself if he's on the way to heaven. Ten feet ain't a great distance until you're underwater and hungry for air and your lungs are about to explode: little Raeburn is suffering on all three counts.

Fortunately, before he swallows his tongue and enough water to drown, he cracks the top of the water and turns his wild flinging arms into a wind-mill dog paddle. He gasps for air and chokes on phlegm and dirty water until an alert lifeguard grabs him up slaps the hell out of his back, sets him on the pool deck and then proceeds to scold his twelve-year-old sister, Delores. She's been given the impossible job of watching Raeburn by an incidental mother and seizes this moment to turn her pent-up wrath on him.

He ignores both of them with no concerned effort while he finishes coughing up the bottom of the pool. He's been warned time and again to stay out of deep water. But, little Raeburn continues to ignore good advice from anyone that might have his best interest at heart. It's a bad habit he will never break; an ingrained, tragic flaw.

~

The more they stare at one another, the more intense the desire builds in Raeburn to possess her, in every aspect and connotation of the word—desire, insane desire, conjures in his mind and body, but he is practiced at his art and restrains his emotions. Calm and unruffled—a placid, noon-day summer pond, that conceals a seething volcano, below the surface. He lies in wait, perched on his white, vinyl-strapped chair—playing it cool.

~

He doesn't want to get involved because he knows they're screaming at each other about him and his latest antic and because he hates screaming and because he hates the thought of owning up to his own imperfections. He knows he ought to stand up for his mother. But, truth be told his only interest in life lies in protecting his own skin from the wrath of God and his daddy's whiskey-soaked anger, especially his daddy's whisky-soaked anger, which always leaves him black and blue and full of hate. At six years old he has already begun to understand the slow painful process of alone.

~

Raeburn puts his dark glasses on, to protect his eyes from the sun and Raven's fire and fixes on her movements in the way a predatory cat, maybe, a tiger—yes, definitely a tiger, eyes the prey it's curious about and toying with and waiting patiently to devour in his own good time. But, not yet, not until the hunger grows large enough, will he swoop in.

The most thrilling part of the hunt is to enjoy the beauty and grace of the prey being stalked: the more elusive, the rarer, the more exciting the chase. Raeburn knows this from experience and knows it will make his final conquest more succulent and satisfying. He also knows she will come to him and that makes him feel powerful and in control.

She is practiced too and knows all this and more—knows that, ultimately, she'll be the one to dine, at her leisure, on the bones she picks clean, all in good time; but, first, the feast.

~

Raeburn has been out on the trail for three nights and two days searching for his quarry. It's his first big game hunt in The East and so far it's a miserable affair. The monsoons have, unexpectedly, come early so the dry, malaria-free camp he was promised in the brochure has turned into a morose, muddy bog. However, his Indian guide, Patel, has proved a reliable and knowledgeable companion so he has decided to tough it out and come home with a trophy chinkara.

Hard-won experience tells him, now is the time to harness every discipline he possesses to overcome an impatient attitude. Prey this delicate is easily frightened to flight.

The blood runs high in his veins as Raeburn closes on his intended target. Some would say it's nerves or fear—he knows better; it's an intense excitement born of natural, innate desire to conquer and control. He lives for this moment, the moment when his sights line up and he squeezes the trigger, a triumphant moment with familiar recoil. Then it's done. The result is predictable. Raeburn yawns.

~

Aware of his cavalier attitude, Raven thinks to herself, as she finishes her last lap, we'll see about that you conceited rascal. She takes her time as she strolls up the half-moon, tiled, concrete steps, on the shallow end of the pool, gives him a coy view of her top half, then, smiles to herself as she watches his next reaction, slyly, from the side of her face. She knows he will fall all over himself if he is any kind of man, when her firm ass, barely concealed, in a high cut, skin-tight, one-piece emerges from the water.

~

She has been feeling somewhat neglected, but rather than feel sorry for herself, eleven-year-old Raven has decided to take matters into her own hands. She has learned that in order to survive the chaotic existence of her wealthy, powerful and oft-times irascible parents a charming smile and gentle demeanor are her best tools. It makes the entire household staff and anyone else in her vicinity immediately want to put her under their protection and care. It fills a void and keeps her hunger at bay. It conceals a fierce, but well controlled passion that bubbles barely below her surface.

~

Raeburn sits up at full attention and peers intensely, over the top of his shades, at the most beautiful woman he has ever seen. Flawless; her long legs flow onto the sun deck and she feels his eyes follow the hypnotic sway of her heart-shaped hips; a self-assured, seductive goddess, unembarrassed, without apology, daring him to come steal her. Raven is all grace and long limbs; the very epitome of a Jewish American Princess and he is all dirt-farmer genes and grab-you–by-the-hair-and-haul-your-ass-off-to-bed—it's love at first sight.

Roderick E. Billette

~

His shocked victim writhes high into the air and too late, tries to run, unaware that her heart has exploded and that she is already dead. She collapses and lies in a crumpled heap her life's blood coughed out.

Patel urges caution. This is rhinoceros and big cat country in northern India. The drought which ended mere days ago has left behind innumerable half-starved animals rumbling around in the tall pink-green Baruwa grass on the prowl for fresh meat. Raeburn pushes Patel aside and ignores his warning.

~

Raven bends over, shakes out her flowing black mane innocently, then turns; her eyes get tangled in his and she finds herself, suddenly, a little less assured of the outcome of the game they're playing.

Lean and muscled, his calm look makes her feel something deep down inside—something deep down inside that she'd forgotten about. Lost in the moment, all she wants is to be taken and adored—he is ready to oblige. She walks toward him as he rises from the lounge chair with his hand out. She takes it. They don't exchange words—they don't need to. They don't leave her hotel room for three days.

~

The open elevator descends through the magnificent hanging gardens of the Hyatt-Regency's idea of modern-day Babylon. This is the terraced home away from home of the wealthy and privileged. A frail little girl with a creamy complexion and white-gloved hands emerges in the lobby and shows a big white toothy grin to everyone she meets.

She is wearing her new expensive summer dress with turned down white socks and matching shoes that aunt Sophie bought for her— she is the essence of feminine culture and innocence combined. Raven appears confused and dazed as she looks around for direction, like a deer in the headlamps. It's a well-rehearsed ruse, practiced daily in her full-length mirror, to achieve the goal of having someone constantly at her beck and call to attend her every whim.

~

A week later, Raven, travels north, to finalize a good divorce and a bad marriage leaving Raeburn alone, with his own demons to fight. His marriage is in shambles and has been for a long time; his fault, too much work and too many endless affairs searching for her. Now what?

One part of him hopes she'll return, but another part whispers loudly to his better judgment, it would be better if you never saw her again, in that way she would always remain the perfect encounter—passion in a fool's dream.

But, those thoughts are angst-filled and melancholy. He knows in his heart he must see her again. He also knows when he does, he won't be able keep his lips and hands from running wild. The heat is turned too high. They are seamless lovers; when they make love, they can't tell where one begins and the other ends. It's mind-blowing. It's surreal. It simply is.

~

Abruptly, from nowhere, five hundred pounds of savage death charges: The Bengal has stalked her quarry silently for many hours and is not about to let an interloper have her meal. She brushes by a stunned Raeburn who can't believe he isn't ripped to shreds, lifts her fanged head defiantly, shakes the fresh kill and shatters the earth with a gruesome display as she lays claim to the warm red meat lying in the blood-soaked grass. It's hers and she will have it, at any cost. She is starving. She will not retreat. She is fixed in her intent. She is magnificent.

~

Three months pass. Then, one night, sitting on a red, round-top, stool in the local bar, something catches Raeburn's eye—it forces him to turn his head. Maybe it's her scent, maybe it's her walk or maybe, it's simply her. Raven comes around the corner wearing a big, bold, floppy, straw hat that accentuates her girlish freckles and fresh face—she is possessed of a simple elegance that some women are born with and others die trying to achieve. On this night she has done something unusual and taken a chance on her wardrobe. She feels in every fiber of her body, it's the look a country boy will adore. She's right.

~

As time goes by Raven becomes enthralled with her ability to win people with her reticent yet inviting smile and begins to use it to her advantage long after she has outgrown the little girl's need. It gets her everything she wants and doesn't want. It intrigues men to love her and take care of her and run all over each other to protect her and give her their material possessions but won't allow her to follow her heart to a love she sees in her dreams and knows must exist somewhere.

She knows, because she is intelligent and soulful and can feel it on rare days when she's not running from herself. Unfortunately, she also knows dreams are ephemeral and rarely tell the truth and certainly won't soften her cynical heart.

~

He sets his bourbon and water on the bar and his eyes on her. In that moment, he knows he will be in love with Raven the rest of his life. She looks back at him with a coy laugh and smiles to herself. She knows the hunter has become the prey. She feels a deep rush of satisfaction at winning so easily, but what she fails to realize in that moment is that she's also a victim of her own trap.

She's in love with Raeburn as much as he's in love with her. Neither of them counted on that and it scares them mindless. Both are proud and accustomed to winning this high-stakes game of who steals whose heart and then running like hell. They are mirror images— distorted reflections.

From the first, they're both destined and doomed. Destined to love in a way neither will ever find or know again; doomed, because they come from such different worlds and need such different things. It's apparent: simply look at them and listen to them talk, you know it's true. They speak a language, foreign to each other. God-only-knows, had they been born mutes maybe they'd have had a chance.

But, that's not right, either, because they do say everything to each other in their own ineffable language of looks and touch. They understand each other completely. Perhaps that's the saddest part of all, they know better than anyone else why they're destined to love each other and yet, not travel the road together. It's as though they want everyone including themselves to believe their love for each other is counterfeit and never mattered.

In the beginning, though, they don't think about any of this, they desire only one thing—a place to be alone so they can ravish each other over and over. How curious and short is life. They try to leave tomorrow in the care of tomorrow, but time falls away and sweeps them downstream—flailing; if only they could've gathered themselves long enough to find a weathered bridge to stand upon.

~

Without a second thought as to whether it is prudent or legal or illegal or moral or immoral a hot-tempered and resolute Raeburn throws caution to the wind and puts a well-placed 6.5 magnum round in the tigress's head—another trophy to display. He doesn't give a solitary damn what anyone thinks of his action. He doesn't want to consider that the tiger has a right to stake her claim or that he should let her have her prey or that letting nature take its due course would necessarily result in life. He can't seem to think at all. He seeks no approbation.

~

Small towns hate to let go of good gossip. Mine included.

After the inevitable blow-up, Raven stayed on in Florida and married a man, who could give her the more refined friends and life she desired. No, what I mean to say is the life she needed and must have. I know what she still desires. She isn't fooling anyone.

When her hours are close and confused, and they often are these days, she walks down the winding path in her garden among the daffodils and roses and honeysuckles and sweet-smelling Confederate Jasmine and thinks about Raeburn and absorbs the warm, splintered sunlight that filters through the black cloud, pendent over her heart.

She always wears the same convincing smile, but if you bother to look closer, right at the corner of her eyes, you can see she is lost in a labyrinth of her own devices caught in the sad undertow of a life that should be so much more. So, although you meet her on the path and talk to her perfect white smile and she says, "I have the life I always wanted." Be aware, deep inside her practiced shell, she's wondering to herself… if only.

And Raeburn…he wanders in and out, and up and down, stumbling about as lost as ever, in the dark, un-lit alleys of a town that takes no pity on one such as he, praying he might find the key to the woman that fills his mind, and starves his soul and wonders to himself… if only.

A Dim Road

I fell on hard times recently. I strolled around a corner one golden glowing afternoon, hands in my pockets, whistling a happy tune out, onto the balmy-breezed air, and got knocked on my can by a cold, swift slap of Arctic air.

It turned me up and dropped me on my already too soft head smack in the middle of the cold, wet, metal-grated storm sewer of life.

The blood rushed down to my head. The rotten scent of the sewer went up my nose. And it stank. Damp, dark disgusting I felt dirty all over. The dirty you feel when you know you can never be clean again. The dirty that leaves you abandoned.

~

Where I come from everybody works hard in the Orange groves from daylight until dark all week including half-day Saturdays. The second half of Saturday is for grocery shopping and preparing Sunday meals ahead.

Our traditional day of rest is Sunday. It begins with a big breakfast. Usually salt-cured ham, and grits, and eggs and fresh-baked biscuits covered in Orange blossom honey followed by ten o'clock Sunday School and an eleven o'clock hellfire and brimstone sermon, followed by midday dinner spread out on checkered table cloths dotting the church grounds. By two o'clock Sunday afternoon the gospel singing is in full throat.

Then home for a short nap before we get another good dose of hellfire and brimstone, then early to bed and early to rise Monday morning. And then do it all over again—week after week, year after year.

This routine of life sounds pretty boring, but it has a quiet, reassuring, rhythmic, undercurrent—soothing to hold onto—silent and strong; The sun rising, cozy nights, a mother's love, and a father's hands.

Go to school, make good grades, work hard, get a good job, find a warm, willing woman to love, settle down, make babies, and continue the slow symphony of life you hear all around you.

This is the way I learned it should be. So, naturally I expected it would be.

Everything went according to schedule until I walked around that damned corner.

~

Train tracks are laid straight and strong, but even the mostly carefully laid must rest on a solid bed. If the bed is undermined the direction of the rails is altered and the whole damned train turns into twisted, screeching, carnage—no survivors.

It happened to me in my 33rd year. I was forced out of my cocoon, forced to examine God's reason for me. Time is no friend, but I would like to explain. Some might not be interested, but it's important for me to tell the tale—to get it off my conscious.

I turned up a dim road late in the day on December 23, 1978 to have a little Christmas cheer in private. I was stressed with work. A small swig of a little somethin', somethin' on the way home seemed like a good idea at the time. Benedictine and Brandy was my choice.

Rural northwest Florida is filled with gravel roads that run off here and there and end in grassy pastures. It was on to one of these dim roads I turned; my favorite place for a snort, less than a mile from my house. The road is private and belongs to my uncle.

A Live Oak lives there with a great umbrella canopy and massive, sprawling roots. The giant tree is a good place to stop, and stretch, and take a piss—feel one with nature.

My custom was to sit on the rising, rough bark of a low-slung branch, enjoy my brown liquor and solitude, collect my thoughts for an hour or so, adjust my attitude, climb back into my Olds 98, and then head home to my lovely wife.

But, as I approached my favorite spot on this particular afternoon, there was already a sedan parked under the spreading branches. There are "No Trespassing" signs everywhere and a cattle gate to open before arriving under the tree. So, I was somewhat surprised to find another vehicle already there.

However, if I'd had the room to turn around undetected, I would have. I was looking for privacy, not confrontation. But, since deep drainage ditches follow alongside the road it would have been unwise to attempt a U turn in the tank I was driving.

And to be honest, I was curious. The car under the tree was a brand-new Cadillac, and I wanted to know what kind of person would bring such a fine automobile into such a dusty, desolate spot.

But, wait, the back doors were sprung wide open and the car was rocking in place. Holy shit! The prospect of what I was about to see brought a sly smile to my face and a familiar warm tingle to my manhood. The blood sang brighter in my veins.

I had all kind of smart things in mind to say. I figured from the type of car it was, most likely it would be middle-age adults sneaking out for some afternoon delight. I figured I'd have a little fun, embarrass them, and then drive on a ways to give them time to collect themselves before I turned around.

They'd skedaddle. I'd get my privacy—no harm done.

I let my windows down as I pulled up even with the open doors of the Caddy and inquired innocently. "Can I be of any assistance?"

I times of deep stress and tension, time tends to go into slow motion for me. Sting is finishing "Shape of My Heart" on the radio, the clock on the dash reads 3:15, two bushy-tailed grey squirrels chase each other around the rough bark of the tree trunk, a Semi out on the highway hits his Jake brake, and the woman screams in ecstasy.

Loose gravel flies in all directions as my Olds 98 comes to a sliding halt. The startled woman riding on top of the man is staring straight at me. Our eyes lock. Passion and fear are traced on her face. Permanent pain and rage are etched into mine.

The Morning Edition of the Chronicle tried to make sense of it all. The details were understandably delicate to describe. The readership is, after all, largely church-going Pentecostals.

But, folks love gossip and a good scare. Put those two together and you've got a winner. Parents were warned about letting children see the copy. This warning served to increase the circulation of the country paper to record levels.

The graphic pictures were suppressed. Even a rag like the Chronicle didn't have the stomach for those: A local banker, naked; hung by the neck from a Live Oak branch with his own leather belt— his private parts cut off and stuffed into the mouth of the woman swinging next to him.

The ambulance chasers pleaded me insane. The doctors agreed. Nobody ever proved anything except, that the banker was the judge's brother's, wife's first cousin, once removed.

Death row ain't been such a bad place as folks might think. These last twenty years I've had plenty of privacy and time to think. Lots of people come in and talk. Say they want to hear my side of the story. Say they are sympathetic. Say they want to understand. Hogwash, they're all looking for a book deal at my expense.

I hear confession is good for the soul. So, I confess: I smile whenever I think about Benedictine and Brandy, and close my eyes, and sniff that warm December air, while I sit under a tall, moss-hung branch of a certain Live Oak tree that stands in my uncle's pasture down a one lane, one-way dim road.

SHORT FICTION

A Noir Tale

"Jump."

The fool does. Splat! Six stories down the sidewalk is engraved with his nose and chin.

Detective Jerome saunters over and flips the bloody body over with the toe of his wingtip shoe. "Jesus H. Christ, what a mess." He steps back disgusted. "He nods at his negotiator, Lt. Randy. "Why 'n hell did ya yell jump?"

"Ain't sure."

"Ain't sure?" Detective Jerome stares at the bleach-blond sporting a swollen purple eye snuggled up tight against the Lieutenant. "Who's the broad?"

Lt. Randy jerks a thumb at the mess on the concrete. "His."

Justin

Justin can see her across the crowded, milling, room. So, he turns to his companion, Joyce, and whispers, "Who is that intriguing creature with the short-cropped gray hair?"

Joyce, who is six inches shorter, stands on her tippy-toes to see the slim, muscular lady he is pointing out to her. "Oh, that's Janey Moore. She's the wealthiest woman in town, and a notorious man-eating cougar.

Justin replies, "Fascinating, I must meet her, sometime."

Joyce answers, "Why not now? She's the friend of a friend. I'll introduce you. But I warn you, at forty, you are way too old. Her taste runs to much younger men."

Justin glances back across the room, then at his half-empty wine glass. "Well, I've enjoyed all the bitter shit in this glass I can stand—maybe some other time."

Joyce says, "That, shit, as you call it, is expensive as hell."

"Well, I'm no oenophile, but I know what bitter tastes like. And this is bitter shit." Justin is on a roll. "No reflection on you, Joyce, but these local elitists in their little esoteric enclave bore the hell out of me; everybody standing around trying to act enlightened and knowledgeable and artsy."

Joyce laughs, "I understand, but I live here, and I've got to try and get along with all these assholes." She waves at the room.

Now it's Justin's turn to laugh. "Fair enough, Joyce. Look, it's time for me to make an exit. Enjoy the rest of your evening. And thanks for keeping me company, always nice to see you, sweetheart."

"See you 'round, darlin'."

Justin turns to make his way through the crowded milieu. Someone touches his wrist lightly, but insistently. How strange.

The lady he'd been admiring has approached him. "I saw you staring at me pretty intensely—made me squirm. And that ain't easy. Do I know you? Have we met?"

Justin responds, "No, ma'am, I don't believe I've had the pleasure. Forgive me if I've made you feel a bit uncomfortable. But, I must admit, you do arouse a certain curiosity in me."

The lady purrs, "Aren't you a bit old to be aroused so easily?" She extends a delicate, bejeweled hand. "My name is Janey—what's yours, handsome?"

"Justin, Justin Thyme."

How I Spent My Summer

Dribble, dribble, dribble, the tide rolls in—the tide rolls out. Sand squishes between my toes. The horizon blurs. Blame it on cheap sunglasses—can't be the

Jose Cuervo tossed back for graduation breakfast.

My rented nylon-webbed chair sinks, stuck fast to the wet grainy beach. Salt-surf laps at bell bottoms, casting cold water on hot dreams— time to move up to dryer ground.

I nudge my companion, "Bring the bottle." Another bite of breakfast and morning reveries resume hotter than ever.

Day after day after day, dribble, dribble, dribble, the tide rolls in—the tide rolls out.

Redheads

War-weary, camouflage hats rest with casual, yet somehow reverent, comfort atop eight, tough buzz-cut, mostly sparse, gray heads, the curious, mottled, word "Redhead" barely legible on the wrinkled, brown bands.

Frayed chin straps pulled tight against the back of each man's neck reveal a habit deep-rooted in close range combat and leave the curious onlooker with no room for doubt, these are serious men.

Practiced, measured eyes, unhurried in their deliberation, peer out from under original, soft, ragged brims, determined and crinkle-edged with time; eyes with a fierce memory, four decades old, still capable, of reaching down inside a man with primal intensity and with nothing more than a hooded glance, infuse grim, visceral fear.

These shadowed eyes ever send a message of quiet thunder: we are Rangers, we command your respect, and we are the elite covert group, code name, "Redhead"

The Late Return

Twenty years has passed—twenty years, could it have really been so long? The interior of the homey log cabin remains intact—exactly as he remembers.

Since his last visit he has become an international star, appeared on late night talk shows, 60 minutes and been interviewed by every major news outlet in the world. Everyone needs his time now. It wasn't always so, but she had believed when no one else did.

Now, it's her time—her touch—her attention—the look of love in her eyes—he craves above all. The lamp by her favorite chair is lit—and the one by his too. She must have been reading late—not unusual she keeps a book close at hand most evenings. The book set aside is open.

He has so looked forward to the visit. Her perfume permeates the air. He wants to tell her all about the insane questions his last interviewer had on his mind. Share his real thoughts on the matter, not the glossed over answers they all expect.

He wanders over to the linen closet, left slightly ajar—she was always bad about closing doors. Tide detergent permeates the closet with its own peculiar odor—must be laundry day. The distinct scent of cedar burned in the fireplace distracts his nose. The holiday log—she had remembered.

The air has something else strange in it—permanent sadness. He turns and sniffs—picks up the throw carelessly lying across the back of her reading chair—left there—never moved—left to ward off late night chills. He picks it up and smiles—breathes deeply of her—of her aroma—of her essence infused in the cloth.

This is what he will remember all his days.

POETRY

Heat

Heat!

    Scorched, burning, Heat!

        Wet, sweltering, Heat!

Rising up from the earth; sucking the beginnings of life up out of the rivers and the lakes and the oceans, spreading out across the low, Florida, sky.

Shining!

    Shimmering!

        Hanging suspended above the asphalt.

Looming!

    Dancing!

Lurking!

A specter in the mist, breathing. Heat!

July Sunday mornings so hot our cups run over with fire and brimstone raining down from Pentecostal pulpits—spilling out all over the South.

    Monday mornings—back in the fields

        Salt sweat rolls down on to the hardened muscles, then drips down on to the calloused hands back into the sandy ground.

    Steaming!

Later, the night heat descends, stifling, stick to your sheets, Heat!

Soak your pillow, Heat!

Toss and turn, smoldering, Heat!

Feather beds, glowing in the dark, Heat!

Building higher, Kinetic!

Ready to explode, Heat!

Always, Heat! Endless Heat!

Melting Heat!

Alive!

In my memory forever forged…Heat!

Point of View

There was a young poet named Henderson

who designed clever rhymes and iambic fun

until one day immersed

in a point of view verse

his past, future perfect, presently came undone

A Song Writer's Dilemma

I sat down to write

a song—I confess

took one look around

Lord, what a mess

Clef staff and modu-li

who'd 've guessed?

eighth notes unbound

Oh! How they test

Un-rul-y trebled lines

in measured duress

half-beats and quiet

sort out the rests

as dawn arrives

sight read—fresh—

a lyrical peal—

a poem—success

Dreamers

Thrive on life's quest to turn the world on end

with pen and paper dipped to deeded task

live where dreamers dare 'round the river bend

Poems of sad refrain, of lover's end,

of tragic verse; to avert these, you ask?

Thrive on life's quest to turn the world on end

Whisked lines of iambic meter wend

down ice-capped mountain streams to glen and cask

live where dreamers dare 'round the river bend

Verse in a mad rush is the current trend;

Anonymous ideas that unmask

thrive on life's quest to turn the world on end

Note the ways of the aged sage; why defend

a drunkard's heaven in a whiskey flask?

Live where dreamers dare 'round the river bend

Thrive on life's quest to turn the world on end

Rejoice anew; in truth and knowledge bask.

Do what cowards daren't do; fight, upend,

live where dreamers dare 'round the river bend

Jake and the Train

Chug-A-Chug-A-Chug-A-Lug! Whoo, Whoo! Clang, Clang! The large model train goes round and round the outdoor track. Jake sits back on his haunches mesmerized by the clanking of wheels and the shrill whistles coming from the engines. No! Wait! He is not mesmerized rather he's contemplating and calculating, a fascinated young engineer on the job figuring how it all works and more importantly how to make it better.

This would seem like an ordinary run of the mill day except this is Sunday and Jake only made it to three years of age two months ago.

Night Cloak

Night has hung her cloak upon the setting sun

and followed the lovers into a close-breathed room.

Passion envelopes the pores of the shadows on the bed

wet kisses—permanent tattoos

Thoughts on Stars

For Irma B. Williams: A birthday celebration

Coruscations flung far and wide

across the universe

rest high above

in heaven's grace...magically

Magnificent fires burning bright

far flung passions

in ebon skies

dying to give us light...magically

Until on one rare occasion

a humble star

veiled at birth

was borne to earth...magically

Roderick E. Billette

An incredible living star

that illumes each room

she passes through

clearly, sweetly…magically

This star, my sister

is a light in the world.

My Irma, may you

shine a hundred more…magically

Jannie

A lady rare I came to know

one of sweet and suppl'd soul

a wanderer of the earthly Globe

a seeker of love each and ev'ry day

of Certain Truth beyond the veil

a world of light beyond the pale

Royal Haiku

Silk worm spins cocoon

On regal branch

Emperor emerges

The Pact

Time has flung upon the wind,
fickle promises no one spends
Come my dear—share this truth with me!
Come my love—make a pact with me—
larceny is an old noble name—
stealing hearts will be our game

Away, away, to the sea with me
down to ships with cargoes laden
high with spice—intense delight
Come my love—run away with me

Come my sweet—swindle sin with me:
venomous veracity—
calumnious capacity
Away, away on a lark with me
round earth's poles to central bliss
passionate lips possess our kisses
Come my sweet—steal the night with me

Roderick E. Billette

Come my dear—make merry with me

Whether or no you play the game

Jilted Jane or Royal Train

Away, away to Gilead's balm we'll flee

Butterflies

Cocoons escape their skin,

turn into Butterflies and then;

fly away high,

high into the sky.

Co-written with: Miss Sara Miriam Garza

St. Augustine

I went to St. Augustine last summer to try on a Panama hat and fish in the waves and play in the white sands of Vilano Beach with pals Shane and Stefanie and Rebecca and a one-eyed Dungeness crab.

A Yeti filled with sunscreen, color-print towels, pistachios, and a tent mashed flat, trails a borrowed cast net stashed inside a five-gallon pail across a narrow foot bridge to prove sixty still has a fling or two left.

A twist, a heave, a circular fan, and a tasty school of Whiting fins, and gills roils and wriggles, and wrangles—snagged fresh from the brisk, briny sea.

~

Rebecca, blue eyes wide and excited, climbs onto her boogie board

in the sudsy surf, while her daddy, Shane, scans the horizon and tap, tap, taps in time to the rise and fall of the crashing spray—a practiced protocol.

A gentle push and swoosh and she's off—a mermaid on top o' the sea up and away on the inbound tide, a scream, a slide, and a wild free ride—

Oh! to be four again—what grace, agility and peer-less nobility, follow white spray and unbound curls into the shallow, receding foam.

Properly salted—a memory snared in Papa's net of gratitude.

Afternoon at the Beach

Brilliant sun, blue sky

clouds float in careless circles

fingers sift fine sand

— *for my friend Jan (Jannie) Cloutier*

Roderick E. Billette

Sunday Morning Fishing

Will the morning still smell so sweet when I am no longer here?

Will the quiet fog still envelope the lake on Sunday mornings?

Will someone else still fish the edge?

While the sweet pungent odor of snow on the Orange trees casts

a wet blanket into the Florida air

I sure hope so for my children's sake

my grandchildren's pleasure and

for the memories I must surely carry into heaven's realm

a place and time I loved dear with all my heart and soul and being!

The Otters

Jack Lanier and I have netted our fair share of speckled perch this January trolling minnows and beetle spins on thin filament lines cast from our newly arrived blessing—a center console Scout.

Gutted and cleaned, leftover heads and fins and hearts and roe are tossed into the lake; food for friendly otters swimming somersaults in the shallow, rhythmic, cattails swaying 'round the dock.

For supper—fish, filleted and boned with a razor-sharp Rapala grace our menu and plenty of whoppers and collards and red-ripe tomatoes choice and crisp from Homer's dew-laden, hillside garden.

Greens, gossip and gratitude simmer in the warm kitchen as Joy sets the table.

Grand Sara Miriam, happy to help, bows her head, and turns thanks over our fare share served up from the cutting bench.

Roderick E. Billette

Lake Ola Fishing

Will the foreign future taste so sweet

in another's mouth

where the Minn Kota hums and whirs

and churns the glass?

Will a large mouth bass leap to eat

in silver shallows

while lily pads dance and bloom

on Lake Ola air?

Will forgetful fog blanket the morn

or recall the past

where I fished the weeded sandy sweep

with my Zebco 404?

Well-loved, let loose this earthly realm

of word and rhyme

Why? It's time to cast a better line;

a grandchild's smile.

Will you honor the host, the Planet Blue,

the unborn child?

Where I go, with all my heart and soul—heaven,

I pray it be so!

After Love

Yellow Moon! Looking

Down from the mountain

Inebriated, confused, walking among

Frost scattered ashes

Why the Moon Smiles

Oh, swift messenger, stark slivered nascent moon deign

extend enchantment 'cross salubrious spring vales

moss tangled beam, diffused purposed shroud awake

grope, pierce; Yes! Chivalrous shaft stroke sweet magnolia's

spread-eagled limbs; elegant elixir obey

solemn, imbued, breathless, broach inscrutable space

raptur'd lovers enfold; revel in each embrace!

Lost Love

Oh Ghost! Formless

Piercing

Alive

Soulless! Craving
Light

Eternal

Gasping! Clawing

Lost

Love

Grace

Silent night of heaven's grace lead on to morn
'neath fern-limbed Cypress bathed in rustling moss
soothe the desire of tomorrow's fresh heart
speak of cloistered love and angels winged
stroke my ear and whisper quiet gibbous moon
age-old answers mortal ken too long denied
softly sift God's illumed immutable truths
expose wisdom's face; dawn-lit, sound and clear
silent night of grace—unfolded, exhaled

How Will You Be

Lord Death showed and knocked upon my door

but a moment more, Sir, I implored

I've letters left to write and loved ones

yet to be

and children and their children that mean

the world to me

Please, Sir, that draft is dreadful cold

what will they do come the morrow?

How will they be?

Yet Death, insistent, beat upon my weakened door

please, a moment more, Sir, I implored

I've a song to write and prose incomplete

yet to be

And my old lover and worse my old dog who's been

the world to me

Come, Sir, don't act so callous, so cold

what will they do come the morrow?

How will they be?

But Death, unrepentant, waltzed through my door

no more time for you, Sir, he underscored

my laundry list has many wrongs to write and souls

yet to be

Prayers and pleadings sewn late mean little in

the world to me

Come, Sir, your name appears in bold

If not today, when—the morrow

How will you be?

January

January—, oh! gray January

layered cloud upon cloud,

upon mood, upon...

dark mood.

Cold uninviting January

I am a child of the sun

I am a child of...

light moods.

January—oh! gray January

Roderick E. Billette

"Strings on Fire"

Yesterday Fast Denny played,

harmonious and profound,

youth burned—desire obeyed.

Passionate, loud, proud

strings on fire; a dash of

music and lyric the Big Shadow cast.

He sang, he soared, he danced.

A heart full of romance

gone in less than a glance

In Memoriam—

Michael "Fast Denny" Robinson

Shelter and Shade

Sixty years past a young man, with a shovel sharp and sound,

planted a sapling of sprouted promise and avian song,

a solid spindle nourished by dew and rain and sun in turn,

in good time grew stout and tall, full of acorn seed,

shelter and shade for progeny.

Fifty years passed—a hired hand, with an axe sharp and sound

felled that solace of splendid promise and oxygen strong.

Atop the remnant root ravaged by rot and blight and sawdust churn,

there he stood, stout and tall, full of manly seed,

shelter and shade for progeny.

Many years past, my wise ol' dad, limbs askew and bark unbound,

bid us adieu in a purchased promise of mahogany and bronze.

Thru weathered winds and dreams awry, what remains, what returns?

Mother Nature, stout and tall, full of newborn seed,

shelter and shade for progeny.

Dedicated to the memory of my father, R.K. Billette

The Drunken Parade

We come and we go—
incandescent,
incessant patterns, marching,
blindly,
generation upon generation,
burning brightly,
weaving in and out of time—
a drunken parade.

The Passage

Time is passing slowly

Passing slowly by

Passing slowly by

Bye Bye Time

Slowly passing

Slowly passing

Bye Bye Time

Passing slowly by

Bye Bye me!

Life's End

Lone-ly dim-lit road

Sun sets, horizon hazy

Lost; night approaches

ONE HOT ESSAY

THE BONFIRE

Hard to believe, my father has been gone for over ten years. He was such a force for good in his community and the world. He is sorely missed. In his last year we discussed many things as fathers and sons will: religion, politics, family and finances. But the subject of one man hating another for the color of his skin and his beliefs was his favorite soap box. I'm not sure what he would have thought had he lived to see the trade towers fall and the subsequent great divide in the years that have followed.

This bonfire narrative is his—an oral story passed on to me. Therefore, this account is not verbatim. I will, however, make a humble attempt to capture the essence of my father's concern regarding the state of affairs in America, his position on race relations, how we got this far and the direction he feels we should consider.

~

A huge bonfire created of rotting ideas, injustice, and callous indifference to our humanity was created when men began to own other men. They named the institution slavery. Every soul put in chains caused the pile to swell larger and stink to high heaven.

In addition, cunning laws of indentured servitude were put into place to steal the time and labor of other human beings. This, of course, was done to satisfy needs and egos at the expense of freedom. Since these decrees were the law of the land the edicts helped ensure social acceptance of insidious institutions.

From the beginning, the stink was putrid and like all organic matter generated heat as the rotten crop decayed. The deeper the inhumanity was piled the hotter the core became. From time to time, over the centuries the intense heat and friction inside this pile of slavery generated brief flames of freedom and reduced its size. Yet the institution remained all down the centuries quelled by the powers of starvation and intimidation.

Yet the fires of freedom breathed. Independence found a home in America where, stoked by brave men and women, liberty thrived in the face of overwhelming odds. Free will would not be denied.

A civil conflagration followed that promised to set all men free and make them equal under the law. The oxygen of souls yearning to be free fed the smoldering, festering pyre and the pile of corruption burned hot with freedom. The rot of slavery had been exposed and supposedly expunged from the land.

The institution of slavery began its reluctant retreat. However, mistrust and hate on both sides continued to add more refuse and fuel to a new bonfire every person of conscience had hoped destroyed. This pile was more dangerous than the first. This new rot was built on fresh smoldering ashes. The ground never cooled.

This assured folks with an axe to grind they would have ample years to stir hot hatred between the races back to life for their own mean-spirited gain. The 1960s brought another civil conflagration. This conflagration in the country promised once again to finish the job and end inequality in our great land forever. Brave men and women almost succeeded.

Over the last few years the fire has cooled from time to time, but heaps of grey ash cover hot coals giving a false impression the fires are out. Make no mistake, folks, black, white, red and yellow, walk around the pile every hour of every day pouring words of hate onto the dying heap; words filled with dishonor, bigotry and shame. Our worst instincts fodder for their grist mills of greed and ambition. Pain and hate exist on both sides of the issues.

Too many attempts at civil discussion and difference of opinion degenerate into finger pointing to real or imagined past wrongs. These differences immediately raise the specters of accusation and guilt, which add to the rot. We are preyed on and ravaged by people with no conscience who would like nothing better than to see this rotting pile of prejudice continue forever.

Selfish interests wish to convince us that this is a primal deep-seated misunderstanding between the races—misunderstanding of who we are and what we need and want. A misunderstanding so great that they contend our differences can never be bridged because of too many unreasonable people of all colors and cultures.

These obscene actors continually seek to turn man against man. Peoples of different color and backgrounds fight each other making the puppet master's endgame easier. Fueling the fires of bigotry and disparity is how they profit, how they get re-elected, how they influence and steer our worst impulses from the comfort of their Madison Avenue offices and plush chairs on the airwaves. These rumormongers push the deadliest drug of all, fear: the most universal and accepted form of slavery. Yes, slavery.

As long as we are force-fed by these conspirators we are all less free. Fear stirs the ash heap and keeps the covered coals alive and simmering. This immorality enslaves us all; no matter our color, creed or nationality.

In the depths of my soul, I believe the naysayers are absolutely wrong and absolutely in the minority. The rest of us must and will find the courage to turn away from the past and lay claim to the shared promise of our American heritage.

Dear reader, don't you think the time has arrived to embrace the racial and cultural melting pot that makes us the most unique and free people of the world?

This bonfire metaphor will cause uneasiness and yes, anger among some folks and perhaps this analogy will be interpreted as an over simplification of what every one of us knows is a complex and vexing situation, but since Abraham turned one son out into the desert and gave the other son his house and name, conflict among different peoples of the Earth has been the order of the day.

I don't pretend to be wise enough to solve this world-wide problem and definitely don't presume I understand all sides of the suffering, denigration and hopelessness enslaved people of all races have endured, and continue to endure, heaped upon their souls.

I only wish to present a human view of what I see as blight on the entire human race. We are all armed with words and hurt feelings, but my hope is that the next words we choose to speak to each other will be kind and understanding and healing.

This essay is intended to focus attention on the deceitful purveyors of distorted information; the media and politicians who in the name of disingenuous unity continue to stir and stoke the fires of racism for their own personal ambition.

They cloak their controversial meandering of wrongs in concealed conciliatory tones, words that belie their intent to play one side against the other--their only interests to increase ratings, line their pockets and win at the polls.

The time is ripe for peace loving people of all ages, all walks of life and all races to say, "No more, we've had enough of being told we can't resolve our differences amicably and agreeably." We as a nation of free people must embrace our collective wisdom. Let us not continue to be used. We are capable of thinking forward for ourselves.

Let us awaken from being followers of the perverse. America is a great nation with untold potential for all. We must move past the idea that men and women of different color seek different things.

I believe we all seek the same freedom to dream and plan, to seek a bright future, a future where our progeny fulfill hopes and dreams, a future where we live up to the promise of a free society. Free in every sense of the word. Free to think and build and prosper without hate and prejudice. Free to walk the path of light.

So, what, you say? You haven't said anything new. I agree. I am only one voice pointing to the obvious. I dream that when enough voices join mine, not in hate, not with an agenda but with the idea that all men have the right to pursue their lives freely, peacefully and with dignity we will become an inexorable choir; a relentless, unshakable force.

Let us once and for all scatter the hot coals of enslavement to the four winds. Perhaps then our song of unity will bury the hate and ignoble disgrace of human being pitted against human being. Perhaps then the road to Eden may once again become ours together—the journey home not so far.

Perhaps then all children—your children and my children, will carry the noble torch of humanity forward in peaceful purpose and conciliation. Perhaps then we may truly inherit the grace of God and build heaven for all in America, a shining example the rest of planet Earth must surely seek to emulate.

Biography

Roderick E. Billette lives in the historic community of Tangerine, Florida, surrounded by a variety of left-over Southern in-laws, and out-laws. He studied English at Clemson University.

He has been known to jump from a perfectly good airplane, dive on a coral reef, and on occasion, saddle up a pony and go for a ride. In his spare time, Roderick is a musician, songwriter, and poet.

His current Southern Gothic trilogy: The Diary of Dakota Johnson, Beginnings, and Reunion are available at select bookstores and online at Amazon.com

For more information about Roderick's work, including poetry, short stories and song lyrics, please visit: Rodbillette.com